BOYS ARE YUCKO!

Other Apple paperbacks
you will enjoy:

Cassie Bowen Takes Witch Lessons
by Anna Grossnickle Hines

Summer Stories
by Nola Thacker

The Hot and Cold Summer
by Johanna Hurwitz

Good-bye, My Wishing Star
by Vicki Grove

Too Many Murphys
by Colleen O'Shaughnessy McKenna

Katie and Those Boys
by Martha Tolles

BOYS ARE YUCKO!

Anna Grossnickle Hines

Inside illustrations by Patricia Henderson Lincoln

AN
APPLE
PAPERBACK

SCHOLASTIC INC.
New York Toronto London Auckland Sydney

ISBN 0-590-43109-9

12 11 10 9 8 7 6 5 4 3 2   0 1 2 3 4 5/9

Printed in the U.S.A.   40

First Scholastic printing, June 1990

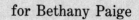
for Bethany Paige

Contents

End of Summer

Cassie Bowen read the last words on the last page of the mystery and closed the book with a snap. Sprawled on an old quilt on the floor of the tree house, she folded her arms across the book, rested her chin on them, and let out a long sigh. It was a hot afternoon. One of the hottest all summer.

She glanced up at Agatha Gifford, who was leaning against the railing of the tree house, still engrossed in her reading. Cassie rolled over and stared up into the leaves overhead. Lemonade, she thought. Ice-cold lemonade! Boy, would that taste good right now.

At the familiar squeak and gentle bump of a screen door opening and closing, Cassie sat up. Agatha's grandmother was coming toward their hideaway, carrying a frosty jar in one hand and a basket in the other.

"Granny's a regular mind reader," Cassie said, lowering the elevator box to the ground.

"Snack time," Mrs. Gifford called out.

"You're amazing. Just when I know I'm thirsty, there you are with something to drink."

"The Amazing Granny Gifford. Knows all! Sees all!" Agatha said with a flourish of her hand. She helped Cassie wind the rope to hoist the box, now heavy with the jar and the basket, up to the tree house. Mrs. Gifford steadied the box until it was out of reach.

"Ummm! Thanks, Granny," Agatha said.

"Yes, thanks a bunch, Granny." Cassie caught hold of the box and guided it to the tree house floor. She liked calling Agatha's grandmother Granny, as Agatha did. The first time it had been sort of a mistake, like calling your teacher Mommy when you're in first grade, but it had felt good. Agatha and Mrs. Gifford liked it, too, so Cassie kept it up. She smiled to herself, thinking that until a few months ago she had been afraid of Agatha's grandmother because of some of her odd ways.

"Do you want to come up and join us?" Agatha asked.

"Oh, no. No thank you. I'm too old for tree house climbing." Mrs. Gifford tilted her head back and shaded her eyes. "I'll go have my lemonade with Roberto."

"Tell him we said hello," Cassie called, teasing the old woman about her favorite houseplant.

"Maybe Roberto would like to come up here sometime," Agatha joked.

"Well now, he just might," Mrs. Gifford chuckled. "He doesn't get to see much of the world from the dining room. I should ask him if he'd like to visit." With a wave to the girls, she headed back to the house.

Cassie poured lemonade into two of the three cups she found in the basket. She handed one to Agatha and took a long drink from the other. "Perfect," she said. "Your grandmother is wonderful."

"You've said that about a million times already."

"I know," admitted Cassie. "It's just that I thought this was going to be such a horrible summer. I'd have been stuck at home with my stupid brother for a baby-sitter if Granny hadn't said I could come over here all the time. It's really been great, you know?"

"For me too," Agatha agreed readily. "I would have had to spend all my time alone . . . except for Granny, I mean."

"And I'd probably have had to tag along everywhere after Joel, watching him play baseball and show off for the girls. Boy is he getting weird now that he's fourteen! Boys! Yuck."

Another familiar door slam was followed by the sound of sneakers pounding across the grass.

"Speaking of boys . . . " Agatha said.

"Hi, guys," called a voice.

"Hi, Jimmy," the girls answered.

3

"He always knows when it's snack time." Cassie poured lemonade into the third cup and refilled her own.

Jimmy Thompson's dark, curly head appeared over the edge of the floor, his brown eyes shining and a paper bag in his teeth. Agatha shifted to make room as he pulled himself onto the platform and dropped his bag to the floor. "Comic books," he said. "What's up?"

Jimmy had helped the girls build the tree house. Having him help had not been their first choice, but unfortunately the tree grew on Jimmy's side of the fence. So even though the tree house was technically in the Giffords' backyard, the tree was technically in the Thompsons'. Jimmy's entrance was up the trunk on his side. The girls climbed up a ladder on Agatha's side. And for a boy, Jimmy wasn't so bad.

"Just reading," Agatha replied. She picked up her book and leaned back against the railing.

"Lemonade?" Cassie held out a cup with one hand as she lifted the napkin off Granny's basket with the other. "Oh, boy! Peanut butter cookies!" She took one and passed the basket.

Jimmy grabbed a handful and settled himself in the corner. He picked out a comic book and tossed the bag to Cassie. "Boy, is it hot. I can't even believe school starts Monday."

"I'm glad," Cassie said. "I think I'm going to like fifth grade." She looked at Agatha, who was reading again.

The two of them had already decided what to wear on the first day of school. Cassie's cousin had sent a really cute blue dress, and when they were shopping Agatha found one that looked sort of like it. They were going to wear those dresses with new shoes, new socks, and new underwear. They'd also shopped together for school supplies and bought matching notebooks and pens that wrote in three colors.

Cassie loved first days with everything new and fresh. A whole new school year beginning—it was exciting. She reached for another cookie. Of course, a new beginning meant being nervous, too. A lot could go wrong.

She nibbled her cookie and pulled a comic book out of Jimmy's bag. She flipped through it looking at the pictures of Huey, Dewey and Louie at summer camp, but her mind wouldn't stay on the words.

"Do you think we'll be in the same class?" Cassie asked.

"I don't know," Jimmy shrugged, reaching for the cookie basket.

He wasn't the one Cassie was concerned about. She nudged Agatha and repeated her question. "Do you think we'll be in the same class?"

"I hope so." Agatha held up crossed fingers to show she meant it.

"Do you think we'll get Mr. Williams or that new teacher?" asked Jimmy.

"I don't know," Agatha said.

"I hope we get the new one. Don't you?"

Agatha shuddered. "Mr. Williams scares me. Remember that time we heard him hollering all the way down the hall? I'd hate to be in his class."

"Yeah, you'd have to be crazy to want Williams," Jimmy agreed.

Cassie chuckled as a mean thought came to her. "I hope Sylvia gets him. She deserves him."

"They deserve each other!" Jimmy exclaimed.

"My mom said the new teacher came into the bookstore yesterday," Cassie said. "She bought some stuff for her class. My mom said she was really nice. Pretty, too."

"She'll be prettier than Mr. Williams, that's for sure," Agatha joked. They all laughed.

"She probably hates boys. Lots of women teachers hate boys," said Jimmy.

"That's because boys are so bad," Cassie teased.

"Ha ha!" Jimmy retorted. "You're so funny that you're putting me to sleep." He stretched out full length on the tree house floor and closed his eyes.

Cassie yawned and checked her watch. "A nap sounds like a good idea, but I have to go home. It's my turn to start dinner." She scooted over to the ladder and started down.

"What are you going to make?" Agatha asked with a mixture of amazement and pride.

"Macaroni and cheese. It's easy." Cassie couldn't help sounding a tiny bit smug. She knew Agatha was impressed that Cassie's mother had given her so much responsibility in the kitchen this summer.

Sometimes all that work was a pain, but usually Cassie felt pretty good about it. She didn't know any other kids who could cook when they weren't even ten years old yet.

She wouldn't be ten for another month. Her mother worked full time in a bookstore, and it made Cassie feel more grown-up to be able to help at home. She was tired of feeling like the family baby who had to be taken care of by everybody else all the time. "So long."

"See you tomorrow," Agatha called.

"Yeah, tomorrow," Jimmy said. "Three more days of freedom before . . . you know . . . "

Cassie walked the short distance home, stopping to check the mailbox, which was empty, before she went inside. Joel was already flopped across the sofa watching television. "Any mail?" Cassie asked.

"Not for you."

She looked through the stack of envelopes on the counter anyway. There really should be a letter for her . . . but there wasn't. She didn't understand it. It had been such a long time since her dad had written, over two months now, and nearly a year since she'd last seen him.

She washed her hands and put the water on to boil for the macaroni. As she grated the cheese she thought about his last letter. He had said he had a new job in California and that he had been to the beach a few times. He said she'd love the ocean, and he promised to teach her how to body surf someday.

He'd also promised to write again soon. He sure had a funny idea about what soon was. Sometimes she was so angry with him for not being married to Mom anymore, for not ever coming to see her, and for not writing, that she almost felt like she hated him.

And there were times when she closed her eyes and wasn't sure she'd remember what he looked like without pictures to remind her.

Would he really take her to the ocean someday and teach her to body surf—whatever that was? He had taught her to swim up at the lake. She remembered him holding his hands under her when she first learned to float. That was when she was little. Last summer they had swum together all the way to the buoy in the deep water. Cassie hadn't been sure she could make it, but he'd coaxed her bit by bit until she had.

She opened a can of green beans, dumped them into a pan, and set the pan on the stove. Then she got out the fresh vegetables for a salad. As she washed them, she wondered if her dad ever thought of those times. Did he miss her like Mom said? Or had he mostly forgotten about her?

He'd be surprised to see how much she'd grown and how helpful she was. How would he like having a big responsible daughter? This summer she could swim to the buoy easily.

As Cassie was finishing the salad, her mother came in the back door. "Oh, look at that! That salad looks beautiful, Cassie." She gave Cassie a little hug.

"I'll just go change and be back to help you get it on the table."

Quickly Cassie set the table. That was really Joel's job when she cooked, and normally she would make a fuss about his not doing it. But tonight Cassie felt like doing everything herself. She wanted her mother to be especially proud of her.

She put the food on the table and called Joel to dinner just as her mother came back into the kitchen.

Mrs. Bowen smiled at her daughter. "Thank you, Cassie. You've done a great job."

"I'd have set the table." Joel scowled at his sister. "Why didn't you call me?"

Cassie looked at him innocently but couldn't keep a trace of superiority out of her voice. "You knew it was time. You could have come without being called."

"Now don't spoil a nice thing," Mrs. Bowen warned. "Cassie set the table tonight. You can do *her* a favor sometime."

Cassie felt good in spite of the dirty looks her brother sent her. She knew she'd pay later, but she was still proud of having prepared the whole dinner herself.

Rainbows for Luck

Cassie woke up and kicked off the sheet. It was already so hot! She flopped over, hanging her head off the edge of the bed. Two round eyes peered up at her. "Sorry, PeeWee," she muttered, reaching for her stuffed bear. "I didn't mean to push you out." She tucked him under her chin and closed her eyes again. But it was too late and too hot for sleeping.

I wonder if I'll get a letter today, she thought. She turned her bear around so she could look at him. "What do you think, PeeWee? Shall I write to him again? I could just sort of remind him about my birthday." Cassie stared pensively for a moment, remembering her father's promise. She jumped up abruptly and plunked PeeWee on the bed. "That's what I'll do. Then he'll know for sure that we're expecting him."

She found a pencil in her desk drawer but hesitated over the choice of paper. Should she use the rainbow stationary or the one with kittens? Remembering that rainbows are supposed to bring good luck, she decided on that, slipped a piece onto her clipboard, and settled back on the bed.

Dear Daddy,

How are you? I am fine except I miss you. I know you are busy, but I hope you write soon. How is California? How is the beach? We didn't get to go to the lake very much this summer, but I took swimming lessons at the pool.

I mostly go to my friend Agatha's house. We go up in our tree house that I already told you about in another letter, and read and play and stuff. School is starting next week. I'll be in fifth grade, but I guess you knew that already.

I hope you are planning to come for my birthday next month. You promised that you would never miss anything important in my life, even if you lived far away. I know you had to miss Joel's birthday because you just got a new job then and you missed Christmas, but that isn't as important as a birthday. It's for everybody, and a birthday is just for one person.

So please come and please write soon. I love you.

Love,
Cassie

P.S. PeeWee misses you, too. That's the bear you gave me last year. Remember? It will be his birthday, too.

Cassie heard her mother in the bathroom, getting ready for work. Then there were footsteps in the hall and Mrs. Bowen knocked on Cassie's door. Cassie turned her letter over.

"You up, sweetie?" Her mother opened the door and stuck her head in.

"Sort of up."

"Joel's still sleeping. He might as well take advantage of his last Friday with no school. Next week it will be up and at 'em." Mrs. Bowen sat on the edge of the bed and rubbed her daughter's back. "It's going to be hot today. I'm glad the bookstore is air-conditioned. That doesn't help you though, does it?"

"It's not so bad up in the tree house," Cassie said. "There's usually a breeze."

"What are you writing so early in the morning?"

Cassie looked down at her clipboard.

"Another letter to your father?" her mother guessed.

Cassie nodded. "Why do you think he never answers me?"

"I don't know, Cassie."

"Do you really think he misses me?"

"I'm sure of it. Who wouldn't miss you?" Mrs. Bowen kissed her daughter on the top of the head. "I was thinking, isn't the roller rink air-conditioned? How about if I give you some money and you can treat Agatha this afternoon. I'll give you enough for a soda or ice cream, too." She took the money from her purse and put it on Cassie's desk.

"Thanks, Mom." Cassie thought how great it would be to join the other kids at the rink for a sort of end-of-the-summer fling.

"Well, you deserve it. Call me later, okay?" She blew Cassie a kiss from the doorway.

"Okay. Have a good day, Mom."

Cassie added a row of X's and O's to the bottom of her letter and decorated it with hearts at the ends of the rainbows. She addressed the envelope, slipped the letter inside, and tossed it onto her desk. "That should do it," she said, hopping out of bed.

She slipped on a pair of shorts, a top, and her sandals, and hurried into the bathroom. Back in her room, she quickly pulled up the sheet and bedspread so it almost looked like she'd made the bed. "There you go PeeWee," she said, propping the bear up on her pillow and shaking her letter in front of him. "Wish me luck."

A quick bowl of cereal and some orange juice and she was out the door. As she turned up the walk at Agatha's house, she saw Mrs. Gifford bent over her zinnias. "Hi," Cassie called.

"Hello to you." The old woman put a hand on her back as she straightened up, tilting her head back so she could see out from under the brim of her big floppy hat. Her face was flushed from working in the heat. "You look chipper this morning."

"And you look busy," Cassie replied cheerfully. "Is Agatha inside?"

"No. I'm right here," called a voice from the middle of the garden. Agatha stood up, her hands full of weeds.

"You go on now," said Mrs. Gifford with a wave at her granddaughter. "You've been a big help. I'm going to quit in a minute myself. Too hot to do much more." She wiped her forehead with the back of her hand, leaving a smudge.

"Want to go to the post office with me?" Cassie asked, as Agatha deposited her weeds in a basket and brushed her hands off. "I want to get this letter in the mail this morning."

"Can I, Granny?" Agatha asked.

"All right. You could do an errand for me while you're at it. We'll need some bread for lunch. Take the change out of the sugar bowl and stop at the market on your way home."

"My mom gave me some money so we can both go roller-skating." Cassie followed Agatha into the house. "Want to do that after lunch?"

"Sure. It will be cool at the rink."

"It's Joel's turn to cook, so we can stay all afternoon if we want. I'll bet we can even get a ride home with my mom."

"Great!" Agatha washed her hands, then counted out enough change for a loaf of bread.

The post office was only about three blocks away, right next to the grocery store and across from the park. They'd gone there often over the summer, sometimes on an errand for Mrs. Gifford or to pick up something Cassie's mother forgot to get for dinner. Sometimes to buy Popsicles or to play in the park.

Cassie held her letter tightly in her hand.

"Who's it for?" Agatha asked.

"What?" Cassie said.

"The letter."

"My dad."

"Did he write to you?" Agatha's voice brightened hopefully.

"Not yet."

Agatha linked her arm through Cassie's and they walked in silence for a while.

"I asked him to come for my birthday," Cassie explained.

"Do you think he will?"

Cassie nodded. "He promised that he would never ever miss anything important in my life, and a birthday is important. We always have really special ones at our house. I get to have whatever I want for dinner and whatever kind of cake I want, and then the whole family does whatever I want to do. This year my birthday is on Sunday and the whole day will be mine. Mom won't even have to work."

"What do you want to do?" Agatha asked.

"Go up to the lake," Cassie responded without the least hesitation. "We'll take a picnic and stay all day like we used to before he left. Maybe we'll even rent a boat. That's what we did last year for my birthday. That's when Daddy gave me PeeWee."

"Birthdays were really special with my family, too," Agatha said. "My mom made the prettiest cakes you ever saw." She smiled wistfully and Cassie squeezed her hand. Agatha's parents had been killed the year before in an automobile accident.

"Last year my sister baked me a cake and all, and she invited my friends so I could have a little party," Agatha went on. "But as soon as everybody went home, we both just started crying. That was right before I came to live with Granny."

"I'll bet Granny will make your next birthday fun," Cassie said.

Agatha nodded. "We can invite Roberto." They grinned at each other.

"I'm really glad you came to live here," Cassie said after a while. "You're the best best friend I ever had."

"You, too."

They reached the post office, and as Cassie pulled the door open, she had a wonderful thought. "I want you to come to my birthday picnic, too!"

"But it's just for your family," Agatha protested, catching the door and following Cassie into the post office.

"No. It's my day and I get to have whatever I

want, and I want you to come. So you'll come, right?"

"I guess so." Agatha smiled.

"Good!" Cassie poked her envelope through the mail slot with an air of finality. "That will make it perfect!"

Skating Trouble

As the girls were preparing to leave for the skating rink, they heard a familiar "Hallo-o-o?" coming from the tree house.

"Shall we invite him?" Agatha asked.

Cassie shrugged. "Sure. Why not?"

It took Jimmy just a couple of minutes to get ready, and the three set out for the rink together.

As they neared the entrance, Cassie saw Stacy, who had been in their fourth-grade class, approaching from the other direction. Stacy waved excitedly and slipped in just ahead of them.

It was nice and cool inside. That's probably why there are so many kids here, Cassie thought. That and the fact that it was the last free Friday afternoon before school started. She waited in line for skates behind Jimmy and Agatha.

Stacy got hers and winked pointedly at Cassie as

she hurried to the edge of the rink. Puzzled, Cassie watched Stacy wave to get Brenda's attention. Brenda caught hold of Sylvia's arm and they skated over to the edge of the arena.

Cassie's back stiffened. Brenda had been her best friend until last spring when their fourth-grade teacher had paired Cassie with Agatha, and Brenda with Sylvia, to work on a class project. Then Brenda had started acting just as mean and snotty as Sylvia, especially toward Agatha and her grandmother.

Stacy said something to Sylvia and Brenda, and all three looked around at Cassie. Quickly Cassie turned away and stepped up to the counter to tell the lady her shoe size. Out of the corner of her eye, she saw Brenda and Sylvia skate off as Stacy bent over to put on her skates.

"Thanks," Cassie said when the lady handed her a pair. She sat down on the bench between Agatha and Jimmy, slipped her feet out of her sandals, and pulled on the heavy socks she had borrowed from Agatha.

Across from her, Stacy finished tying up her laces and flashed Cassie another big grin, as if they shared a secret or something. Cassie smiled back uneasily. Stacy was making her nervous.

Jimmy finished putting on his skates and took off. "Catch me if you can," he called over his shoulder as he zipped away.

"Pretty cute," said Stacy.

"What?" Cassie didn't have the slightest idea what Stacy meant.

"Not what! Who! And you know who I mean."

Cassie and Agatha looked at each other.

"No we don't," said Agatha.

"Jimmy!" Stacy said. "He's so-o-o-o cute!"

Cassie and Agatha rolled their eyes. Stacy was too much! They got up and followed her onto the floor, joining the flow of circling skaters.

Jimmy came up behind them. "Race you!" he challenged. Cassie and Agatha took off after him. Cassie lagged behind, but even with Jimmy's head start Agatha passed him. She was a good skater.

Out of breath, the three rolled into the low side wall. "She beat you," Cassie taunted, shaking a finger at Jimmy.

"Well, *you* didn't!" Jimmy defended, "and you never will!"

Cassie heard laughter and looked up to see Stacy, Brenda, and Sylvia gliding by. Sylvia was pointing at them.

Jimmy zoomed off, and Cassie and Agatha went around at a slower pace.

"Show me how you go backwards again," Cassie asked.

Agatha skated out ahead, setting a good steady pace, and then sort of lifted herself up, twisting her body around as she pivoted on her front wheels. She ended up facing backwards.

Cassie tried to imitate her, but the heel of one foot caught the toe of the other and she fell. *Splat!* Right in the middle of all those skaters! The same thing had happened the last time she'd skated.

Agatha came back to lend a hand as Cassie scrambled to her feet. "I think I have too many wheels on these things," she joked as they took off.

Cassie gave the tricky maneuver another try. She was concentrating on keeping her feet a safe distance apart when Brenda and Sylvia skated up behind them, chanting.

"Cassie loves Jimmy! Jimmy loves Cassie! Oooo la la!"

Cassie glared at them, but before she could say anything, her left wheels bumped into her right skate and down she fell again. They went right on by, singing those stupid words.

Cassie picked herself up and skated after them. "Stop it. Come on, you guys! Cut it out! It's not true!"

Sylvia turned. "Oh? Is he Agatha's boyfriend then?"

"No! He isn't anybody's boyfriend. He's just . . ."

"What's wrong with him being your boyfriend?" Brenda teased. "He's kind of cute."

"He is not! He's just a stupid boy! Boys are yucko!" Cassie said.

Brenda and Sylvia looked at each other and grinned. "Cassie loves Jimmy! Jimmy loves Cassie!" They skated off laughing and chanting.

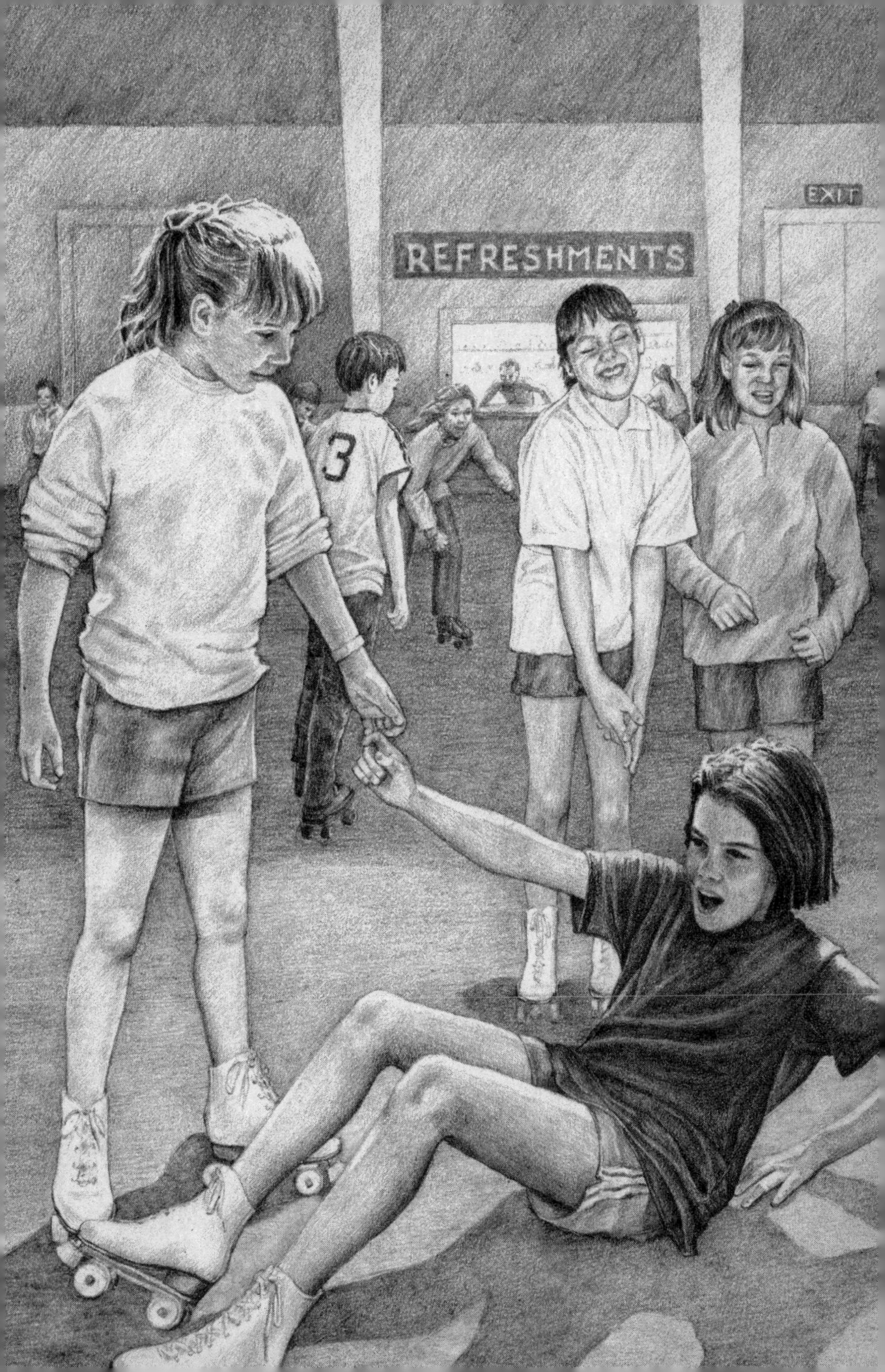
REFRESHMENTS
EXIT
3

"I do not like Jimmy! I don't like any boys!" Cassie muttered under her breath, letting them get well ahead of her.

"What's the matter?" Agatha asked, as she and Stacy caught up to Cassie.

"Those two again!" Cassie pointed. "They make me so mad! They're saying 'Cassie loves Jimmy! Oooo la la!' "

"So? They're just jealous," said Stacy. "Jimmy's really cute. I think you're lucky. I wouldn't mind if he liked me."

"Jimmy doesn't like me!"

"Then why did he come skating with you?"

"Because he just wanted to come skating. Look, he lives behind Agatha's grandmother, you know. So this summer we built this tree house in his tree, in the part that sticks over Agatha's backyard, and we had to let him help because it was his tree."

"So-o-o-o," said Stacy suggestively, "you built a tree house together. That sounds real cozy."

"Come on, Stacy. Cut it out!" Cassie fumed.

"Yes," said Agatha, "he's just my neighbor. Just a boy. So big deal."

Stacy laughed. Agatha took Cassie's arm and pulled her to the side of the rink. "Let's take a break," she said.

"Good idea. I have money for some soda. Want one, or should we get ice cream instead?"

"Soda," Agatha said. "I'm thirsty."

They got their sodas. Jimmy already had one and motioned for them to sit with him.

"Better not," Cassie said, catching Agatha's arm and pulling her to another table.

They watched the skaters go around the rink as they sipped the icy drinks. Stacy was with Brenda and Sylvia, and they all laughed and gestured at Cassie and Agatha every time they went by.

"Just ignore them," Agatha advised.

Cassie stretched her legs out on the bench and leaned against the outside of the arena wall. The view wasn't terribly exciting: a few old posters of famous skaters, dusty and ragged around the edges; the snack-bar menu that had new prices pasted on top of the old ones; and one of about a dozen lists of "Rules of the Rink." Still, Cassie felt herself calming down as she drank her Coke.

"Hey, Cassie! How come you don't sit with your boyfriend?" Three girls' voices shouted all at once.

Cassie's face flushed. She glanced at Jimmy to see if he had heard, but he was talking to Mike.

"They're really being dumb." Agatha looked disgusted.

Cassie sucked the last of her drink into her straw. "Are you ready? Come on. Let's skate."

Around they went once, twice, almost three times. "I'm going to try going backwards again," Cassie called. She let some people pass by, leaving a nice clear space. Then she set her pace and gave a little jump, twisting herself around.

"I did it! Agatha, look! I did it! I'm skating backwards!"

"I knew you could!"

Cassie glanced up to see the other three girls catching up to them. She didn't like the look in their eyes and wished she were facing forward so she could go fast and get away from them. But going backwards, it was all she could do to stay on her feet.

At Sylvia's signal they all three burst out chanting, "Cassie and Jimmy sitting in a tree, K-I-S-S-I-N-G! First comes love. Then comes marriage. Then comes Jimmy with a baby carriage!"

"Thanks a lot, Stacy!" Cassie shouted, grabbing the rail and letting them go by. Agatha doubled back to her. "I hope they all get Mr. Williams," Cassie muttered.

Agatha nodded and offered her hand. "Let's go around backwards together."

With Agatha helping for balance, Cassie got off to another successful start. She felt a wave of gratitude for Agatha's friendship as they circled the rink together. If they could just be in the same class this year it would be all right, and if they got that nice new teacher instead of Mr. Williams, it would be great.

First Day

Monday morning! Cassie jumped out of bed and quickly put on the blue dress. In minutes she had finished her morning chores, eaten a piece of toast, and was kissing her mother good-bye.

"There's plenty of time, Cassie," said Mrs. Bowen. "Wouldn't you like a bowl of cereal or an egg or something?"

"No thanks. I'm not hungry," Cassie insisted, starting for the door.

"Why are you leaving so early? No one will even be there yet."

"I'm going over to Agatha's first so we can go all the way together."

"Are you sure they want you over there at this hour?"

"Mo-om!" Cassie faced her mother with a look of

exasperation. "We planned this. Agatha is expecting me." She stepped out and let the door swing shut.

"Well, have a good day," Mrs. Bowen called.

Cassie was soon at the Gifford house, where Agatha, in her almost-matching dress, was just finishing her breakfast.

"Would you like something, Cassie dear?" Mrs. Gifford offered. "Some juice or tea?"

"No thanks."

"How about a nice warm muffin?"

"Better have one," Agatha urged. "They're really good."

"Thank you," Cassie said, accepting the muffin.

Agatha took another one too. "Can we eat these on the way, Granny?"

"What's the hurry, dear?"

"We have to see if we got in the same class."

"Yes," said Cassie. "We're dying to find out."

"Well, I wouldn't want to be the cause of your untimely expiration," Mrs. Gifford said. "Go along, get on out of here. And good luck!"

"Oh, I hope! I hope! I hope!" Cassie said, crossing as many fingers as she could and still managing to hold on her half-eaten muffin.

"Me too! We have to get the same class." Agatha held up her own crossed fingers. "Even if it's Williams."

They hurried to the school grounds. Quite a few

kids were there already. Some younger ones were with their mothers. One little boy brushed his pale blond hair out of his eyes, his lower lip quivering slightly, as he watched others hurrying in all directions. The girls stopped to help.

"What grade are you in?" Cassie asked gently.

"First," he answered.

"It's okay. We'll take you," said Agatha. They took his hands and walked him over to one of the first-grade rooms.

"Just go on in there," Cassie prompted. "The teacher is real nice. She'll take care of you."

But the boy held back until the girls went in with him. As soon as the teacher greeted him, they hurried out of the room. "Bye-bye. Have fun!" they called.

"Okay, now us!" Cassie sighed. Off they went to the upper-grade rooms. Outside the doors, kids were gathered around looking at the lists of names. Mr. Williams's was the first fifth-grade room they came to. Cassie ran her finger down through the names beginning with *B. Bowen, Cassie* wasn't on the list. "I'm not in Williams's class," she said. "So far, so good."

"Cassie," a familiar voice called, "you're not in that class. You've got the new teacher, like me."

Cassie and Agatha turned to see Stacy standing in front of the next room. They went back to the list. Cassie's finger continued down through the *G*'s.

"I'm not here either," Agatha said excitedly. "Neither of us has Williams!"

"We're together!" Cassie exclaimed. They hugged each other exuberantly, then ran over to the other list.

"I told you. See, there you are, right there." Stacy pointed to Cassie's name.

"And there I am," whooped Agatha. "Oh, good, good, good!"

"Who else is in this class?" Cassie asked, looking over the list.

"Brenda," Stacy said. "But not Sylvia. She's got Williams. Poor Sylvia."

"Yes, poor, poor Sylvia." Cassie pretended to swoon. Agatha grinned.

Stacy didn't pay any attention. "Jimmy's in our class, and Randy, and Mike. All the cute boys except Joshua. We're definitely in the best class."

More and more kids were coming up to check the lists. Cassie, Agatha, and Stacy moved aside to make room. Brenda and Sylvia arrived together.

Cassie nudged Agatha and pointed. Brenda and Sylvia were both wearing dresses! Last year, when Agatha was new, they had been really mean to her because she wore dresses to school. Everyone else wore jeans, even when it was hot.

After she had become friends with Agatha, Cassie started wearing a dress once in a while, too. By the end of the year, a few other girls were wearing dresses. Now lots of them were, including Sylvia and Brenda!

"Brenda, you're with us in the new teacher's class," Stacy called out. "But you've got Williams, Sylvia."

Sylvia and Brenda hurried to check the lists for themselves. "Gross!" Sylvia said. "Ugh! Williams! Nobody's in there. I'm going to get changed to your class. I'll have my mom call the school."

Brenda put an arm around her. "If you can't get changed then maybe I can get changed to Williams. At least we'd be in there together."

Stacy was sympathetic. "Would they really let you change, do you think?"

"Of course they will," Sylvia said. "All I have to do is get my mother to make a big fuss about how I'm being deprived of my friends at this crucial stage in my life, or something. They like to keep the parents happy, you know. They change kids all the time."

"Who have they changed?" Cassie wasn't about to say so, but she couldn't help hoping that Sylvia was wrong.

Sylvia took the question as a challenge. "Lots of people," she said pointedly. "What do you care, anyway?"

"I don't care," Cassie lied. "I just couldn't think of anybody who's ever switched. That's all."

"Of course you don't care," said Sylvia. "You've

already got your best friend and your lover boy in class with you."

"I don't have a lover boy." Cassie tried to keep her voice calm.

"You can say whatever you like," Sylvia gloated. "We know the truth, don't we?" She looked at Brenda and Stacy, and they nodded uncomfortably.

"I think I need a drink of water." Cassie took Agatha's arm and walked away. "What a jerk!" she said.

"I hope she can't get changed," said Agatha.

"You and me both." Cassie took a sip of water, though she wasn't actually thirsty.

"Hey Cassie! Agatha!" Jimmy called out from down the corridor. He hustled toward them. "We did it! We all got the new teacher. Have you seen her yet?"

The girls shook their heads. "Have you?" Agatha asked.

"Yeah! She's real young and pretty. Now let's just hope she's not mean," he said, "and we'll have a good year."

"I hope she's fair," Agatha said.

"Yeah, and that she has a good sense of humor and isn't a grump," Cassie added.

"I hope she doesn't make us do embarrassing projects," Jimmy said, "like making up plays from the stories in the reading book. Yuck!"

"I liked that one," Agatha said.

"Me too," said Cassie, remembering that it was because Mr. Garner had made her work on the play with Agatha that they had become friends. "I hope we do lots of projects. They're more fun than regular work."

The bell rang and the three of them started walking toward their classroom.

"Especially when you get to have partners," Agatha said.

"I like some projects," Jimmy said, "just not embarrassing ones."

The new teacher was standing at her desk in the corner of the room talking with a couple of girls. She was pretty and young, Cassie noted, just as Jimmy had said.

Brenda and Stacy took seats directly behind Agatha and Cassie. Cassie tried not to notice their giggling. She glanced at Agatha, who rolled her eyes and shook her head. Cassie knew she meant, "Don't let them bother you."

A soft chant started up behind her. "Cassie and Jimmy sitting in a tree, K-I-S-S-I-N-G! First comes love. Then comes marriage. Then comes Jimmy with a baby carriage!"

"Come on," Cassie pleaded. "He's not my boyfriend."

"Oh! He must be Agatha's boyfriend then," Brenda said. And she and Stacy immediately switched to, "Agatha and Jimmy sitting in a tree, K-I-S-S-I-N-G!"

"He's not my boyfriend either," Agatha said. "He's just my neighbor. You two are just being Sylvia's little jerks."

Before anyone could say anything else, the teacher called out, "Good morning!" All over the room, conversations stopped and heads turned toward the front.

"Good morning," she repeated, smiling pleasantly. "Welcome to the fifth grade. My name is Ms. Jeffers, and I'm sure you know by now that I'll be your teacher this year. The kind of class we have will be pretty much up to you. It will depend on how you behave and how hard you work. There is a lot to learn in fifth grade, but if we all cooperate and work together, I'm sure we can have fun doing it. I have some ideas, but I'm anxious to get to know each of you and hear some of your ideas and expectations for this year as well.

"I'd like you to think about that while I call the roll. Then we'll make a list and discuss the possibilities."

Cassie opened her notebook and wrote, *I'm glad we got her!*

So am I! Agatha wrote in her own notebook.

After taking roll, Ms. Jeffers called on them one at a time and listed their ideas on the front board. Some kids suggested neat things, like doing real science experiments and putting on a play with costumes and scenery and everything. Others suggested boring things, like studying the dinosaurs, which they had already done in second grade, or impossible things like going to Mars. Ms. Jeffers wrote them all down, no matter how stupid or outrageous they sounded.

When the board was full, the class began discussing which ideas might actually be possible. People got so excited they stopped waiting for turns and started shouting to be heard over one another. Ms. Jeffers gave up trying to lead the discussion. She leaned against the edge of her desk and watched.

Cassie bent toward Agatha and asked, "Why doesn't she do something?"

Agatha shrugged. "Maybe this won't be such a great class after all."

Cassie nodded and slumped in her seat.

Ms. Jeffers watched silently as the chaos continued.

Finally, one boy shouted, "Why don't you tell everyone to shut up?"

Suddenly the room was quiet. Everyone waited to see what Ms. Jeffers would do. Cassie sat up straight.

"I think you just did," Ms. Jeffers said. "I told you that the kind of class this will be is up to you."

"We need some rules," Brenda said.

"How many agree that we need rules?" Ms. Jeffers asked. Everyone raised their hands.

"What rules do you think we need?" She moved over to the empty chalkboard at the side of the room.

Cassie raised her hand, and Ms. Jeffers nodded. "Take turns talking so we can hear each other."

"How many agree that that would be a good rule?" asked Ms. Jeffers. All the hands went up. Ms. Jeffers wrote it on the side board.

Other rules were suggested and voted on, including "Keep your hands and feet to yourself" and "No name calling." The list ended up being very similar to the rules the teachers had made up in third and fourth grades, but Cassie liked the idea of having a say.

There should be a rule that says, "No saying So-and-so loves So-and-so," she wrote, slipping the note to Agatha.

"Good one," agreed Agatha, but neither was about to suggest it out loud.

By recess the list was complete and all had promised to abide by it.

"She's smart," Cassie whispered as she got out of her seat.

Agatha nodded. "I think I'm going to like being in this class."

"Definitely!"

They hung back, letting Brenda and Stacy run ahead to find Sylvia. By keeping an eye out, Cassie and Agatha managed to avoid the other three for the entire recess.

But lunchtime was a different story. Sylvia had picked up a new friend by then, and all four of them chanted the silly verse, first with Cassie's name, then Agatha's. Cassie and Agatha were glad when it was time to go inside. If the playground was going to be like that every day, this year would be the pits, even if they were together and had a wonderful teacher.

Maybe Yes, Maybe No

On Friday morning Stacy joined Cassie and Agatha and some of the other girls from their class at the tetherball pole. Waiting in line behind Stacy, Cassie asked, "Did Sylvia get mad at you?"

"No," Stacy said, "I just got tired of her whining and feeling sorry for herself all the time."

Cassie nodded. Sylvia had not managed to change classrooms and had made a great show of her torment all week. Stacy and Brenda had been her most sympathetic audience.

Then at lunch recess on Monday Brenda was in the tetherball line, too. Cassie figured Sylvia was absent, until she saw her with another girl. Sylvia, obviously snubbing Brenda, steered her new friend to a different game.

Brenda sulked, and Stacy tried to console her.

"Forget it, Brenda. Sylvia just has to be the queen bee and have all the attention."

Cassie felt sorry for Brenda even though she sort of thought Brenda deserved it. Brenda had always gone along with it when Sylvia picked on somebody else. Now she was finding out what it felt like.

A couple days later, when Cassie and Agatha were walking home, Brenda and Stacy caught up to them. But instead of going on by, as Brenda did when she was alone, she and Stacy stayed right behind so the four girls were more or less walking together.

"Hi," Stacy said cheerfully.

"Hi," Cassie and Agatha responded, glancing uneasily at one another.

"So, how's your boyfriend?" Stacy crooned.

Cassie's heart sank. Not that stupid stuff again! "I told you, he's not my boyfriend."

"Must be Agatha's then. Right Agatha?" coaxed Stacy with a silly sort of grin.

"Maybe yes, maybe no," Agatha said. "Why? Are you jealous?"

Cassie gaped at Agatha in surprise. Did she really like Jimmy? Agatha winked at her.

"Maybe yes, maybe no," teased Stacy.

"Definitely yes!" said Brenda, giggling.

"You shut up!" Stacy objected, but she laughed, too. She hit Brenda playfully in the arm.

"Really?" asked Cassie. "You like Jimmy Thompson?"

"Jimmy and about five others," Brenda said. She ducked as Stacy swung at her again.

"You should talk! You like Randy Maple!" said Stacy.

Brenda punched her. "I do not! Don't believe her."

"You do too! You said so at recess yesterday!"

"I just agreed with you that he's cute."

"Sure, sure," Stacy mocked.

"Okay, so I said it. Big deal. You still like more boys than I do," Brenda said. "You wish you were the one sitting in the tree with Jimmy, 'K-I-S-S-I-N-G!' "

"So? What's so bad about that?" Stacy grinned.

"Yuck!" Cassie said.

"So if you don't like Jimmy, who do you like?" asked Stacy.

"Nobody!" Cassie looked at Stacy like she was out of her mind.

Stacy turned to Agatha. "Come on, who does she like really?"

"Nobody that I know of," Agatha said.

"What about you?" Brenda asked.

"Same goes for me," said Agatha.

"Well, if neither of you really likes Jimmy, would you do me a big favor?"

"Depends on what it is," Agatha said cautiously.

"Right," Cassie agreed.

"Just ask him who he likes," said Stacy.

"Ask him if he likes Stacy." Brenda put her hand

by her mouth as if telling them a big secret. Stacy punched her and laughed.

"I don't know." Cassie hesitated. "We don't talk about stuff like that."

"What kind of stuff do you talk about?" Stacy asked.

"I don't know. We just read comic books and play cards sometimes," Cassie said.

"We talk about the tree house and school. Stuff like that," Agatha added.

"I'd like to come up in your tree house with Jimmy sometime!" Stacy rolled her eyes.

"Stacy and Jimmy sitting in the tree . . ." Brenda started. Stacy giggled.

"Would you just ask him, please?" Stacy pleaded. "Just sort of casually, you know."

"Ask him if he likes her for a friend or a girl-friend," coached Brenda.

"All right, all right! We'll ask him," said Cassie.

As they approached the corner where Cassie turned off, she looked over at Agatha. "You coming?"

"Do you just have to change your clothes or what?"

Sometimes Cassie had other chores to do after school, but today she shook her head. "I don't even have to change today. I just want to check the mail."

"Okay, I'll come with you."

Cassie turned to the other girls. "See you tomorrow."

"Don't forget to ask him," Brenda called.

"Today," added Stacy.

"We'll ask him today if he comes over, but if he doesn't, you'll have to wait." Cassie backed down the street. "Bye."

"Bye. Don't forget!"

"So long," Brenda said.

Cassie turned around and the corners of her mouth twitched. "Maybe yes, maybe no," she said in a funny little way.

Agatha grinned. "Stacy is just boy crazy."

"You can say that again. Yucko!" Cassie opened her mailbox and peered inside. "Well, it's not nothing today, anyway." She pulled out a stack of envelopes and catalogs.

She sorted anxiously through the pile. "Mrs. Jean Bowen, Occupant, Ms. Jean Bowen, Mr. Gregory Bowen." She paused over that one. It was sort of odd, but comforting, that occasionally mail still arrived addressed to her father.

The last two envelopes were addressed to Ms. Jean Bowen. Cassie shut the box with a bang, walked quickly to the house, and unlocked the door. She tossed the mail onto the kitchen counter and stared out the window.

Agatha put a hand on Cassie's shoulder. "Maybe it will come tomorrow."

"Come on," Cassie said. "Let's go over to your house."

Mrs. Gifford had grape juice and bran muffins waiting. When they finished their snack, the girls decided to play Parcheesi in the tree house. Agatha wrapped a muffin in a napkin and took it along in case Jimmy came over. He liked her grandmother's bran muffins almost as much as he liked her cookies.

Cassie climbed up first and was pulling the elevator box up when they heard Jimmy's back door slam. "Guess we'll have to ask him," she said.

Agatha nodded. "You do it."

"No, you. You're his neighbor."

Agatha unfolded the game board. "That doesn't make any difference. You've known him longer."

"Hallooo?" Jimmy called from the bottom of the tree.

"Hallooo, yourself!" Cassie answered.

He pulled himself up over the edge. "Hi. What are you playing?"

"Parcheesi," Agatha said. "Want to play?"

"Sure, for a while. Mike's coming over later."

Agatha handed him the muffin.

"Wow! Thanks!"

"What color do you want? Agatha's blue and I'm green."

"I'll take red."

"You got it. Okay, Agatha. You start first." Cassie hoped Agatha would understand that she was talking not only about the Parcheesi game but also about asking Jimmy whom he liked.

Agatha either didn't get the message or chose to ignore it. She rolled the dice and moved one of her pieces. Cassie cleared her throat, trying to work up her courage. Jimmy and Agatha watched her expectantly.

"Are you going to keep shaking those dice forever, or are you going to take your turn?" Jimmy asked.

Cassie rolled the dice and made her move. Then, between bites of muffin, Jimmy took his turn. Agatha made her second move without a word, and so did Cassie. But on Jimmy's turn she nudged Agatha with her foot and silently mouthed the words, "Ask him."

Agatha shook her head. She threw the dice, made her move, and passed the dice to Cassie, who took a deep breath and grimaced. Agatha nodded toward Jimmy. Jimmy looked from one to the other.

"What?" he asked.

"Nothing," said Cassie. "What do you mean, 'What?'"

"I mean, what's going on?"

"Nothing," Cassie repeated.

"You're sure acting weird."

"No we're not."

"We're supposed to ask you if you like Stacy Dodds," Agatha finally ventured.

Jimmy popped the last bite of muffin into his mouth.

"Well, do you?" Cassie was sort of curious now.

Jimmy chewed and swallowed. "Who wants to know?"

"Stacy."

"She's all right, I guess."

"Well, do you like her for a girlfriend or just for a friend?" Cassie persisted.

"This is stupid," Jimmy announced. "I'm going down to wait for Mike." He backed down the tree trunk.

Agatha was trying not to smile. Cassie tried to stifle a laugh, snorted instead, and they both burst into giggles.

Cassie jumped up and looked down into Jimmy's yard. "Hey, Jimmy," she called, "we think it's stupid, too."

He turned and gave her a quick wave as he disappeared into his house.

The girls fell on each other in the silliest fit of giggles they'd had in a long while.

In school the next day, Cassie and Agatha found Brenda and Stacy waiting for them by the gate.

"Did you ask him?" Brenda called as they walked up.

Stacy punched her. "Not so loud!"

"Oh, sorry," Brenda chortled.

Stacy's eyes were about to pop out of her head. "Well?" she asked anxiously.

Cassie glanced at Agatha and didn't say anything.

"Come on," Stacy said. "Did you ask him or not?"

"We asked him," Cassie said.

"Well, what did he say?" Stacy had a silly grin.

"Does he like her or what?" Brenda coaxed.

"He said he guesses she's all right," Cassie reported. "Right?"

Agatha nodded.

Stacy looked disappointed, but Brenda grabbed Stacy's arm and jumped up and down. "Oh-h-h! He likes you! I knew he liked you. See, didn't I tell you?"

"Do you really think so?" Stacy brightened a little.

Just then Jimmy came through the gate. When he saw all four girls watching him, he turned very red, gave a quick little wave, and took off running.

"See?" Brenda said. "I *told* you he likes you."

Agatha raised her eyebrows and Cassie grinned. "See you guys later," she said.

A Dancing Lesson

On Saturday afternoon, Cassie was in her yard eating a sandwich and watching a trail of ants march across the sidewalk. She dropped a crumb in their path. One ant broke from the ranks and began to wrestle with it. That poor ant was really working.

It reminded Cassie of the time her room was being painted and she'd tried to move her mattress alone. She could barely lift one end.

Two more ants had joined the effort of the first when Cassie heard voices. She raised her eyes to see Brenda and Stacy walking toward her. Cassie got to her feet and brushed the dirt off the knees of her pants.

"Hi, Cass," Stacy called. "What are you doing?"

"Nothing." Cassie saw Brenda look down at the

line of ants. They'd probably think watching ants was a dumb thing to do.

"Want to come over to my house and watch 'Star-Dancers' with us?" asked Stacy.

"Stacy's teaching me how to dance," Brenda explained without hesitation. "Her sister taught her."

"I'll show you how, too," Stacy offered. "It's easy and it's fun."

"All right," said Cassie. "I'll go ask my mom."

The girls waited while Cassie ran into her house. She was soon back. "It's okay. I can go."

"Great! We'd better hurry or we'll miss the beginning." Stacy took off running, with Brenda and Cassie at her heels. They ran into her house and straight to the TV. All three stood watching, trying to catch their breath as the set warmed up.

"Oh, good! We made it," Stacy said as the "Star-Dancers" theme song came on. "Let's just watch the first one." She patted the floor on either side of her. "Come on. Sit down."

"Look. See how they do that thing with their arms? My sister showed me how to do that yesterday. I'll teach you. It's like this. See?" Stacy bent her elbows, raised them to shoulder level, circled her fists around each other, lifted the left arm above her head, circled again, and then lifted the right. "Come on, try it."

Brenda imitated the movements, circling and lifting alternate arms in time to the music.

"Right." Stacy nodded. "You've got it." She looked

at Cassie, who wasn't moving. "Come on, Cassie. You try it."

Reluctantly, Cassie made little circles, letting her wrists dangle limply. She felt pretty silly with her hands flapping around in front of her face.

"No. You have to lift up your elbows and make fists. Like this," Stacy corrected.

Cassie laughed self-consciously as Stacy got behind her and pulled her elbows up.

"Now, make fists and do the circles . . . like Brenda is."

Cassie followed instructions, circling and lifting one arm and then the other.

"Yes, that's it. You've got it!"

Cassie smiled, feeling more in control. It was actually sort of fun.

The three of them continued the arm movement until the song ended, getting to their knees so they could twist and sway their upper bodies to the rhythm. During the commercial, Stacy showed them a dance step. It was pretty easy. When the next song came on, they all danced.

"For my birthday, I'm going to have a dance party," Stacy announced. "It's going to be so-o-o great!"

"When's your birthday?" Brenda asked.

"Not until March." Stacy made a long face. "I'll be eleven."

"Mine's in two weeks," Cassie said, "but I'll just be ten."

"Oh! Are you going to have a party?" Stacy asked.

Cassie shook her head. "I'm going to have a family picnic up at the lake."

"Too bad. You should have a party," Stacy declared.

"You didn't have one last year," Brenda reminded Cassie. "So your mom would probably let you have one this year."

"I don't think so. Besides, I don't want a party. I want a family birthday."

"But that's what you had last year," Brenda said. "Why do you want the same thing again? Especially when your dad isn't even there anymore."

Cassie blinked. Brenda was so dense sometimes. She wasn't intentionally mean, like Sylvia. But lots of times she said or did things that were hurtful to others, and she never seemed to realize it.

"A party would be so much fun," Stacy went on.

"My mother doesn't have time to do all the stuff for a party now," Cassie said, still looking at Brenda. "She has to work."

"So have it at your baby-sitter's house," Stacy said. "You could even have it up in the tree house."

Now Cassie gave Stacy her full attention. "Mrs. Gifford isn't my baby-sitter. I don't need a baby-sitter. I just go over there because it's lonely at home and I like to play with Agatha."

"Still," Stacy insisted, "I bet she'd love it if you had your party there. And we could help, couldn't we, Brenda? My mom saved all the decorations from my sister's party last year."

"I don't think it would be such a good idea to have it at the Giffords' house," Brenda said nervously.

"Anyway, we couldn't have it in the tree house," Cassie commented. "It's not big enough."

"Well, in the backyard then," Stacy said. "It could be just a small party. And maybe a couple of people at a time could go up in the tree house."

"Oooo!" Brenda giggled and shook her finger at Stacy, then turned to Cassie. "I'll bet your mom would let you have it at your house on the weekend. You know, just a few kids."

"Yeah," said Stacy, "like just us and Agatha, of course, and maybe Rachel and Angie and a few other people, like Jimmy and Randy and a couple more boys." She grinned at Brenda.

"You really should have a party, Cassie," said Brenda. "It would be so much fun."

"Ask if you can, all right?" Stacy begged.

Cassie scratched her arm, wondering what to do. She didn't know if she wanted a party, especially with boys . . . and with her dad coming. But these two weren't about to take no for an answer. She sighed. "Okay, I'll ask. But listen, don't count on it, okay?"

"Oh, your mom will say yes," Brenda assured her. "Her mom is really nice," she said to Stacy.

"Come on, let's dance some more. Try this one."

Stacy did a tricky little step, crossing one foot in front of the other.

Even Brenda didn't catch on to that the first time, so Stacy did it more slowly, stepping to the side with her left foot, crossing behind with her right, then over and to the side again with her left. "Now you just pick up your right foot, point your toe, then step down and cross behind with your left, over with your right, point." Stacy talked them through it as she demonstrated. "Step, cross back, cross front, point. Good! Okay, now faster!"

"Oh, it's easy! It just looks hard!" Brenda exclaimed.

But Cassie got mixed up, crossed the wrong foot, then nearly tripped when she tried to step to the side. It looked hopeless.

"Here, I'll show you again," Stacy offered.

Cassie shook her head. "I'll just do that other step you showed us. It's easier." Maybe this dancing stuff wasn't going to be so much fun after all.

Birthday Plans

On Monday morning, just as she was about to turn up Agatha's walk, Cassie saw Brenda on the next block. Brenda waved. Cassie waved back and went on inside.

When she came back out with Agatha, Brenda had gone by and was almost at the corner. She was walking slowly. She glanced over her shoulder and slowed down even more.

"Do you think she's waiting for us to catch up?" Agatha asked.

"Maybe."

"Do you want to walk with her?"

Cassie shrugged. "It'd be okay, I guess. She hasn't been so bad since she stopped hanging around Sylvia. Besides, look. Now she's stopped, and if we don't keep going we'll be late."

Brenda had indeed stopped on the corner and was obviously waiting for them to catch up.

Agatha curled her upper lip and wrinkled her nose but kept walking.

"Hi," Brenda called out. "Did you ask your mom?"

Cassie shook her head.

"Ask your mom what?" Agatha wanted to know.

"If she can have a birthday party," Brenda said.

"I thought you wanted to go to the lake," Agatha remarked with surprise.

"I do," said Cassie.

"You can go to the lake anytime," Brenda pointed out. "You can only have a birthday party on your birthday. You'd better ask soon if it's only two weeks away. We have to practice dancing some more, too."

Agatha was very quiet. Cassie wanted to explain, but it was hard in front of Brenda. She tried to give Agatha a reassuring smile, but Agatha wouldn't look at her.

As they approached the school, Stacy ran up to meet them. "Hi, everybody. What did she say, Cassie?"

"She didn't ask yet," Brenda reported.

"Why not? You've got to ask," Stacy said. "A party would be so much fun, and it'll be ages till my birthday. Ask tonight, okay?"

Cassie felt trapped. Everything seemed to be falling apart. Why had she even mentioned her stupid birthday? Why had she gone over to Stacy's in the first place?

"Tonight, okay?" Stacy was incredibly persistent.

Cassie nodded meekly. She wasn't up to arguing.

"Let's all watch 'StarDancers' together again next Saturday, okay? You come this time, too, Agatha. Let's do it, okay?"

Agatha shrugged.

"We'll see," Cassie said.

"Try. Okay?"

Cassie nodded again.

In class she wrote *Please don't be mad* on a scrap of paper and slipped it onto Agatha's desk.

Underneath Cassie's message, Agatha wrote *Who says I'm mad?* She put the paper back on Cassie's desk.

Cassie turned it over to write on the back. *You are my best . . .* She stopped writing and glanced up at Ms. Jeffers. The teacher was looking right at her. Guiltily, Cassie pushed the paper aside and went back to her long division, even though they didn't have any rules about passing notes.

She looked at Agatha out of the corner of her eye. Agatha was looking at her. "Later," Cassie mouthed silently, nodding at the teacher. Agatha turned back to her math.

Long division! Long division! Every problem seemed to go on forever! Math was Cassie's best subject, but it was hard enough when she wasn't distracted by other important things. Today it was impossible. Even though she was only half finished, she was relieved when the bell rang for recess. She'd have to do the rest for homework.

Cassie grabbed Agatha's arm. "Come on. Let's go to the rest room."

"How come you didn't tell me you went over to Brenda's?" Agatha asked.

"I didn't. I went to Stacy's. I was in my yard, and they just came by and asked me to go, so I went. It wasn't any big deal. We just watched 'Star Dancers' on TV and danced a little bit."

"Are you and Brenda going to be friends again, like you used to be?"

"No. Not like we used to be," Cassie said. "Brenda doesn't really understand how I feel about things the way you do."

Agatha still seemed troubled.

"You don't like Brenda at all, do you?" asked Cassie.

"I don't trust her."

"I know," Cassie said. "I don't blame you, either, but she's not so bad now that she's not hanging around with Sylvia."

Agatha nodded. "Now she's just boy crazy, like Stacy."

"Not quite as bad as Stacy, though," said Cassie.

"Nobody is as boy crazy as Stacy!" Agatha said emphatically. She took Cassie's hand as they started across the playground. "Are you really going to have a birthday party?"

"I don't know," Cassie answered. "I'd rather go to the lake, and I don't think I can do both."

"If your dad can't come, then would you want a party?"

"Maybe," Cassie said. "Anyway, my dad *is* going to come, and we *will* have that picnic, and it will be a lot more fun than kids acting goofy all over the place."

"What are you going to tell Brenda and Stacy?"

"I told them I'd talk to my mom. So tonight I'll talk to my mom, then I'll tell them she said no."

"Well, if you do have a party, I'll bet Granny would help. You know how she likes to bake things."

"My birthday is only one week and six days away," Cassie said as she helped her mother clear the table after dinner. Joel had disappeared into his room as soon as he'd finished eating.

"I know," Mrs. Bowen said. "Have you thought about how you want to celebrate it this year?"

"I want to go to the lake again with a picnic."

"We could do that if you want, but wouldn't you rather have a party with some of your friends? I couldn't do anything terribly elaborate, but we could manage a nice little party on Sunday afternoon. I'll bake a cake, get some ice cream and balloons. We could make some decorations and party hats. I saw this cute idea for hats in one of the magazines."

"I'd rather go to the lake," Cassie said.

Mrs. Bowen put down the plates she was carrying and faced her daughter. "Cassie, you know it won't be like last year. I'm afraid it would be a big disappointment to do the same thing with just the three of us."

"It won't be just the three of us," Cassie said quietly. "I want Agatha to come . . . and I wrote to Daddy and . . . and I asked him to come."

"Inviting Agatha is a fine idea," Mrs. Bowen said. "But about your father, honey . . . He hasn't written, has he? Did he say he'd come?"

"He promised me he'd never miss anything important in my life," Cassie said defensively. "Don't you think my birthday is important?"

"Of course I do, Cassie. I just don't want you to be disappointed. What your dad said when he left and what he's done since then . . . I mean, well, I just don't know what's going on with him. I really thought he'd stay in closer contact with you children than he has."

"He promised he'd be here for important things, so he will be," Cassie insisted. "You just don't trust him. That's the problem. But he's coming and he's going to be surprised to see how much I've grown. And he'll be proud of how responsible I am now."

Mrs. Bowen looked anxiously at her daughter. "He should be very proud. I know I am."

Cassie put her arms around her mother, and Mrs. Bowen gave her a good squeeze.

"Cassie?" Mrs. Bowen hesitated. "Cassie, even if

your father does come, going to the lake won't be the same. Maybe it would be better if you and your dad did something different."

"I don't want to do something different." Cassie pulled away from her mother. "I want to do the same thing. You always said we could do whatever we wanted for our birthdays. That's what you said."

"Yes, I did say that, and if you want to go to the lake, we'll go to the lake. But we aren't the same family we were. Your father and I aren't married anymore. I just don't want you to be hurt."

"You're still my mother, aren't you? And Daddy's still my father. So we're the same family! And we can all go to the lake for my birthday. We'll take a picnic and my birthday cake, and we'll rent a boat again. . . ."

"All right, Cassie," Mrs. Bowen said. "We'll go to the lake. If your father comes and wants to go along, that's fine. If he comes and wants to do something else with just you kids . . ."

"He won't want that. It's my birthday, and if I want to go to the lake, then Daddy will want that, too."

Mrs. Bowen seemed about to say something else. But Cassie didn't want to hear any more. "It'll be all right, Mom. You'll see."

Mrs. Bowen turned on the hot water and squeezed some dish soap into the sink, "I have the whole weekend off," she said. "Your birthday is Sunday. What if we save Sunday for the family day, and plan a little party with your friends on Saturday? That way you'll have a nice celebration even . . . while you're waiting for your dad. It will give us something to do."

"Are you sure it wouldn't be too much?" Cassie asked. "I mean making two cakes and everything?"

"Not if you'll help," her mother said. "We could make cupcakes for your party and those hats I was talking about. Besides, I guess you're worth the trouble." She had a funny little grin on her face.

Cassie grinned back. "Okay! Two birthdays! Wait till I tell Agatha. She can come to both, can't she? She can help make the hats and decorations, and she said Granny would like to bake something. She always likes to bake."

"Of course Agatha can come to both," Mrs. Bowen said. "But we can manage the refreshments. Amanda Gifford does so much for us already. Maybe . . ."

"Maybe what?" Cassie asked.

"Nothing," Mrs. Bowen said. "I'll go look for that magazine article as soon as we finish these dishes."

The next morning Cassie leaped up the Giffords' front steps and nearly ran into Agatha coming out the door. "Guess what?" Cassie didn't give her a chance to answer. "I get to have a party *and* go to the lake for my birthday! A picnic at the lake on Sunday, and you can come, *and* a party on Saturday. It was my mom's idea."

"Neat! Who are you going to invite to the party?"

"You. And Stacy and Brenda, I guess. If it's okay with you."

Agatha nodded. "As long as you don't invite Sylvia."

"No way!"

"That's good. How about Jimmy?"

"I don't know. Jimmy's okay, but he's a boy. He probably wouldn't want to come unless I invited some other boys."

"Stacy and Brenda will want you to invite lots of boys," Agatha said, "especially Jimmy."

"I know," Cassie replied, "but it's my party. Maybe I'll just have girls." Cassie counted on her fingers as she named her friends, "You, Stacy, Brenda, and Angie."

"If you invite Angie you'd better invite Rachel."

"Yes, Rachel, and maybe Cheryl and Kristi. That would be eight counting me. That would be good, don't you think?"

"What would be good?" Brenda interrupted, coming up behind them.

"If I invited eight girls to my birthday party," Cassie said. "My Mom said I could have one. I was thinking of you, and Agatha, and Stacy, Angie, Rachel, Kristi, and Cheryl."

"That's seven," Brenda said.

"Well, I'd make eight," Cassie said.

"Oh, yeah. Right. Well, that's good," Brenda said. "And which boys?"

Cassie cringed.

"Oh, look! There's Stacy!" Brenda waved frantically. "Stacy! Guess what? Cassie gets to have a party! Isn't that great?"

"Yeah, great!" Stacy met them as they turned into the school yard. "So, who's invited?"

Cassie named the girls.

Stacy nodded. "Which boys, besides Jimmy, of course?" She looked at Brenda and they both giggled.

"I was just going to invite girls," Cassie said.

"Oh, Cassie! You have to have boys!" Stacy exclaimed. "It would make it much more fun!"

"I don't know," Cassie said. "Boys usually want to do stupid stuff."

"You guys play with Jimmy all the time," Stacy reminded her.

"That's different. It's just one boy, and . . . well, Jimmy's just different."

"Just cuter, that's all!" Stacy giggled. "Come on, Cassie. We could play tapes for dancing and stuff."

"I don't have any tapes."

"Joel does," Agatha said.

Cassie raised her eyebrows. "He'd never let me borrow them."

"I'll bring mine," Stacy offered, "and I could get some of my sister's. She's got tons. I'll borrow her tape player too, unless you have one."

Cassie shook her head. "Just my brother's, and I

don't think he'd let me use that either. Anyway, I don't know how to dance. I don't want to have dancing."

"Sure you do," Brenda said. "Stacy already taught you last Saturday, and we're going to practice again this week. It's easy."

"I don't know. I just don't think I want that kind of party. I don't even like boys."

"Of course you like boys," Stacy said. "You like Jimmy, don't you? For a friend, I mean. Well, that's all you have to do. Just invite some boys, and I'll bring the music and it'll be fun. You don't want to have a silly little baby party with hats and all that junk, do you?"

Actually, Cassie *did* want that kind of party. That was what she was planning, wasn't it? It sounded better than dancing and giggling about boys. But she didn't want everyone getting mad at her, either. She almost wished she wasn't having a party at all.

"I'll talk to my mom," she said as the bell rang and they walked to their classroom. "This has to be a small party because I'm also having my family picnic. I don't know what she'll say."

Lyle Kester

"One tablespoon of mustard," Cassie read from her mother's recipe card for Sloppy Joes. She measured the mustard and stirred it into the mixture simmering on the stove. The French fries were in the oven already, and the salad was made.

She looked through the mail one more time. Two letters for her mother and a catalog from Sears. Cassie sighed, tossed the catalog onto the clean end of the table, and sat down to leaf through it.

Joel came in, empty glass in hand, heading for the refrigerator. "Whew!" he said. "What a mess! You'd better get some of that stuff put away before Mom gets home."

"You'd better mind your own business," Cassie retorted.

"It is my business. I can't set the table until you clean it off."

"What's your big hurry? You never set the table till the last minute anyway."

Joel refilled his glass with grape juice. "It's your head, not mine," he said over his shoulder as he left the room.

Cassie looked around. The catsup bottle and mustard jar sat on the counter alongside the empty soup can and meat wrapper. What was left of the celery and the skin from the onion were on the table with assorted measuring cups and spoons, a knife, and other implements. It was not a sight Mrs. Bowen would like to come home to. She was big on putting things away as you go.

Cassie turned back to the catalog. She'd clean everything up in a minute. She didn't need to have Joel telling her what to do. He thought he could boss her around just because he was fourteen. Well, she'd clean it up when she was ready. She found the girls' section. Mom couldn't afford to buy her very many new clothes but maybe for her birthday . . .

Next thing Cassie knew, her mother was pulling into the driveway. Cassie jumped up and scurried around to put things in order.

"Hi, sweetie," Mrs. Bowen said cheerfully, kissing Cassie on the cheek as she came in. "Dinner smells good." She walked into the living room without a word about the mess.

Cassie continued her rapid cleanup and had the kitchen in order by the time her mother came back.

Mrs. Bowen smiled as she added dressing to the salad and tossed it.

"Did you have a nice day?" she asked.

"Pretty nice," Cassie answered, starting to set the table. "Did you?"

"Yes, it was very nice. I love this weather. It's beginning to feel like fall. Soon the leaves will be turning. I bought some colored paper to make the hats for your party. I put it on your desk with that magazine. Maybe we could start after dinner and finish them up this weekend."

Cassie stirred the Sloppy Joe mixture. The mention of party hats reminded her that she'd promised to talk to her mother about inviting boys. Did she want to include them or not? For that matter, did she want hats? Stacy had said hats were babyish.

"About the hats, I'm not . . . ," Cassie started but was interrupted by the oven timer. "That's for the French fries."

"I'll get them," her mother said. "Dinner's ready, Joel."

He strolled into the kitchen and poured himself a glass of milk.

"Would you pour me some, too?" Cassie asked as he sat down at the table.

"Get your own," he said. "I'm already sitting down."

"I'm still helping with dinner. Besides, I set the table for you."

"You didn't set the table for me. You set the table so you wouldn't get in trouble for not cleaning up your mess. I'd have had it set a long time ago if you'd cleaned up like you're supposed to."

"Well, I could have called you to set it when I was ready, but I didn't, so there!"

"What a little creep!" Joel sputtered.

"All I asked you to do was pour one little glass of milk!"

"All I told you was to get your own milk!"

"Come on, you two," Mrs. Bowen pleaded. "Let's not argue tonight." She put the bowl of French fries on the table and smiled hopefully as she sat down.

Cassie and Joel gaped at their mother in astonishment. She was in an exceptionally good mood.

"This looks good, Cassie." Mrs. Bowen handed her a Sloppy Joe. "You're getting to be quite a little cook. Did you have a good day, Joel?"

"Yes," he said. "Fine." He watched his mother curiously. "Did you?"

Mrs. Bowen smiled. "I had a very good day. What were you saying about the hats, Cassie?"

"Just that . . . well, I'm not so sure I want party hats."

"Oh? I thought you liked the idea." Her mother seemed disappointed.

"Some of the girls think having hats and stuff like that is too babyish."

"We wouldn't want to be too babyish at a ten-year-old's party," her brother teased.

That clinched it! Cassie was definitely not having a baby party for her brother to make jokes about! "The boys probably wouldn't wear them at all," she announced with conviction.

Joel opened his mouth to make another remark, but his mother stopped him with a look.

"I didn't know you planned on inviting any boys," she said.

Cassie twirled a French fry in catsup. "Well, there's Jimmy. Agatha and I play with him sometimes. I thought maybe I'd ask him, and a couple others."

"That would be fine," Mrs. Bowen said. "It's nice that some of your friends are boys. And some of those hats are very appropriate. Besides, I think making them together would be fun. Let's look at the pictures later."

So that was that, Cassie sighed. There would be boys at her party after all. Brenda and Stacy would be happy. Cassie's thoughts were interrupted by a question from her mother. "Do either of you have plans for Friday night?"

Cassie and Joel both shook their heads.

"Would you mind staying alone? I have something I want to do that evening."

"No problem," Joel offered. "I'll stay with the runt."

"I'm not a runt!" Cassie protested.

"Do you have another peace group meeting, or what?" Joel asked.

Mrs. Bowen shook her head.

"Are you going to a movie or something with Carol?" asked Cassie. Carol was a friend of her mother's.

Mrs. Bowen shook her head again. "I've been invited out to dinner."

"By who?" Joel asked.

"Whom," his mother corrected. "By a man I met at the bookstore."

Cassie stared at her mother. This didn't make sense.

"You have a date?" Joel's tone was incredulous.

"I guess you could say that." Mrs. Bowen laughed nervously.

Joel regarded her for a minute, his eyebrows up and his mouth open. Finally, he nodded and smiled slightly. "A date. So who is this guy? What's his name?"

"His name is Lyle Kester. He's a writer."

"Stupid name," Cassie muttered under her breath.

Mrs. Bowen looked quizzically at her daughter.

Joel gave his sister a surreptitious kick and a look that said to go crawl under a rock. Cassie glowered back at him.

"What kind of stuff does he write?" Joel asked.

"Science fiction. He's published two books and lots of magazine stories."

"Neat!" Joel was an avid science-fiction fan.

"I've got a magazine with one of his stories in it, if you'd like to read it," his mother said.

"Yeah," Joel said. "I'd like to."

Cassie stared at the food on her plate. Suddenly she felt more like throwing up than eating. She put a bite of salad in her mouth and chewed. But the longer she chewed the less she felt like swallowing. Finally, she forced the bite down. "May I please be excused?" she asked.

"You've hardly eaten half your dinner," her mother remarked.

"I'm not hungry. Please, may I be excused?"

"All right, sweetie."

Cassie went straight to her room. She sat on the edge of her bed, with her hands in her lap, and stared at the wall. Her mom had a date . . . a date with a man! How could she do that? How could she even think of it? It didn't make any sense. What if her mom had a date when her dad came to visit? That would be just great. They could hardly be a family with an extra man hanging around. Her dad might get really mad . . . like he did that time she accidentally ran her bike into the side of the car. Then her mother would get mad and they'd fight, and then they'd never get back together. Getting back together was what Cassie secretly hoped would happen—that when her dad came to visit, her parents would realize what a terrible mistake they had made and would get married again.

She got up, went into her mother's room, and di-

71

aled Agatha's number. "Hi," she said when Agatha answered. "It's me. I . . . Do you think I could spend the night with you Friday?"

"Sure. I'll ask Granny, but I'm sure she'll say yes. What's going on?"

"Nothing. My mom just has to go somewhere. I don't . . . I don't want to stay here with Joel."

"Okay," Agatha said. "We'll have fun."

"Yeah."

"Cassie?"

"What?"

"What's wrong? You sound . . . you know, sad or something."

Cassie hesitated. "My mom has a date with this guy she met at work."

"She does?" Agatha sounded excited. "That's good, isn't it?"

"No!"

"Why not? Won't she have fun?"

Cassie didn't say anything for a minute. Fun hardly seemed the point. "She can have fun with me and Joel. Besides, my dad is coming back next week . . . for my birthday. I told you."

"But he's not going to stay, is he? Isn't he just going to visit?"

"I don't know. Maybe he'll stay, maybe he won't. But for sure he won't if she's going out on yucky dates. . . . I really don't want to talk about it anymore. I'll see you in school tomorrow, all right?"

"Sure."

"And don't forget to ask about Friday."

"I'll ask right now. See you tomorrow."

"All right. Bye." Cassie hung up the phone and hurried back to her room. "Fun!" she sputtered. "What's going to be fun about it?" She smashed her fist into her pillow, sending PeeWee flying. She picked him up and held him at eye level. "Well, now at least I won't have to be here when that stupid Lyle Kester comes to pick Mom up. At least I won't have to meet him. I hope she has a horrible time."

"Come on. Give Mom a break. She deserves to have some fun once in a while."

Cassie jerked around. Joel was standing in her doorway. "She could have fun with us," she retorted.

"That's not what I mean, and you know it," Joel said. "We're her kids. She needs grown-up friends, too."

"She has Carol and Mrs. Gifford and her friends in the peace group. She doesn't need to go out on any stupid dates!"

"You're such a baby sometimes," Joel said disgustedly. "You don't understand anything."

"I do too! You're the one who doesn't understand! If she starts going on dates then everything will be all messed up when Daddy gets here! And I'm not a baby!"

"When Daddy gets here? What makes you think he's coming?"

"He's coming because it's my birthday," Cassie said firmly.

"Your birthday! You're even stupider than I thought," Joel scoffed. "He didn't come for my birthday, why should he come for yours?"

"Because he promised!"

"Oh yeah? And we all know how great he is at keeping a promise, don't we? When did he make this one?"

"Before he left. He promised he would never miss anything important in my life." Cassie looked at her brother defiantly.

"Before he left he promised a lot of things. Like he was going to write every week and send money so we could go visit him on our vacations. So far, he hasn't been too great at following through, in case you hadn't noticed." Joel's look softened, and the tone of his voice changed. "Listen, Cass. I wouldn't count on this if I were you."

The concern in her brother's manner was harder for Cassie to bear than his scoffing. It was too much! She clenched her fists and ran at him, screaming, "You get out of here! Just get out of here! This is my room!"

"Don't worry, I'm going! I'm going!" Joel raised his arms as a shield and backed up. Cassie slammed her door shut.

Party Hats

Wednesday after school, Cassie checked the mailbox again. Still no letter. She was glad Agatha had gone straight home. She didn't want anyone to see her disappointment, not even her best friend. Agatha had offered to help her make party invitations that afternoon, so Cassie went to her room for paper and envelopes.

The magazine on the desk caught her eye. She thumbed through and found the hats her mother was so crazy about. They weren't that bad. The people wearing them weren't all little kids either. Some were grown-ups and some were even teenagers. They could hardly be called baby hats. Cassie tucked the magazine into her bag and headed for the Gifford house.

Agatha and Mrs. Gifford had rose-hip tea and cookies all ready. Cassie opened up the magazine right away. "Look at these hats. My mother thinks we should make some for the party."

"Oh-h-h! Yeah! That would be fun! Can I help?" Agatha was immediately enthusiastic. "Look. There's a fireman's hat and a cowgirl and . . . Oh-h-h! I like this space hat best."

"You could all wear space hats," joked Mrs. Gifford. "They would go with that way-out music you want to play."

"Hey! That's a good idea," Agatha said. "It could be an outer-space party. We could make flying saucers out of balloons and make it look real neat."

"Right!" said Cassie. "That way it wouldn't be babyish like a little kindergarten party, but it would still be . . . you know . . . fun! Are you going to dance?" Cassie's tone was more serious.

"I don't know," Agatha responded.

"Well, I'm not. At least not with any boys! Yuck! Stacy and Brenda can if they want, but not me."

Mrs. Gifford had an amused smile. "Dancing is perfectly good exercise, besides being a lot of fun."

"Not with boys!" Cassie insisted.

"Someday you'll sing a different tune, young lady. You wait and see." Mrs. Gifford nodded confidently.

"Which boys are you going to invite?" asked Agatha.

"Oh, Jason . . . and Billy . . . ," Cassie slowly and

deliberately named the most annoying boys she could think of.

"Gross!" Agatha exclaimed. "You're kidding, right?"

". . . and Bobby Finch . . ."

"Bobby Finch!" Agatha shrieked. "Isn't he that kid in the other class who's always dive-bombing at the drinking fountain? Now I know you're kidding!"

". . . and Sylvia . . . ," Cassie went on teasing.

"Okay! Okay! That's enough!" Agatha jumped up and clapped a hand over Cassie's mouth.

Mrs. Gifford quickly gathered her teacups out of harm's way. "You two can be rowdy enough for a whole party sometimes!" she declared, but it was obvious that she enjoyed their high-spiritedness.

As soon as the table was cleared, the girls settled down and made the invitations. They decorated them elaborately with spaceships, stars, and planets.

The next morning Cassie left early and waited for Jimmy on the corner.

"Would you give out these invitations for me?" she asked, handing him four envelopes.

"What are they for?"

"My birthday party. Those are the ones for the boys."

Jimmy sorted through, reading the names. "Wow! Spaceships!"

"The whole party is going to have an outer-space

theme. You know, for the decorations and everything."

"Do-do do-do, do-do do-do," Jimmy sang to the "Twilight Zone" tune. He put his arms out and circled around Cassie.

"Come on," she pleaded. "Agatha thought it was a good idea."

"So do I," he said. "Sounds cool."

Walking home from school on Friday, Cassie realized that she was starting to get pretty excited about her party. It was certainly a lot more fun to anticipate than . . . than her mother's date. At least her mother had agreed to Cassie's spending the night with Agatha. She said that way she'd know Cassie and Joel wouldn't be fussing at each other all evening. And I won't have to watch you fussing to get ready, Cassie had thought.

She hesitated as she reached for the door on the mailbox. The excitement of possibly finding a letter was mixed with the fear of being disappointed again. She yanked the door open and pulled out two envelopes, both for her mother. Cassie blinked back her disappointment. There was still a whole week left. A whole week and a day, in fact. And maybe her father was going to surprise her.

She let herself in, dropped the envelopes on the table, and dialed her mother's number at work. Things had been uneasy between them lately. Every day, Mrs. Bowen asked Cassie about school and the Giffords, just like always, but Cassie didn't feel much like talking.

"Hi, Mom," Cassie said when her mother answered. "I'm calling you like you wanted me to."

"Hello, sweetie," Mrs. Bowen said. "How was your day?"

"Okay."

"Did you pass out the invitations you made?"

"Yes. We did that yesterday."

"Can all the kids come? Are they excited?"

"I guess so. Some still have to ask their parents and everything. I'm going to go on over to the Giffords', Mom. So I'll see you tomorrow, okay?"

"All right, Cassie. We'll do those hats when you get home tomorrow. It'll be fun making them together. All right?"

"All right, Mom. Bye."

"Bye-bye, Cassie. Have fun tonight."

Cassie hung up the phone. "Don't you have fun tonight," she muttered. She went into her room to get her overnight case. She had packed most of it the night before and tucked in her nightgown and toothbrush that morning.

She picked up the paper her mom had gotten for the hats and put it in a paper bag. Then she rummaged through her desk drawers for things that might make interesting additions to spaceman hats. Pipe cleaners, bits of foil, stickers, some old confetti.

She added glue and tape, picked up the bag, her suitcase, and PeeWee, and went out the door.

Joel was in the kitchen, pouring himself a glass of milk. "Hi, kid," he said.

"Hi, yourself," Cassie said, walking right past him, "and good-bye."

"Hey, Cassie, wait a minute." He looked at her curiously, hesitating to say what was on his mind. "Uh, you're not still expecting Dad to show up next weekend, are you?"

Cassie glared at him. "If he does, he does." She shrugged.

"Good," said Joel, with a tone of relief. "I just didn't want you to be counting on it so much that you'd get really hurt, you know? I mean, even if you are a pain, you're still my sister."

"You don't have to worry about me. I'll be fine." Cassie turned to go out the door. "Bye."

"Good-bye, and good riddance."

Cassie continued down the walk. "I'll be fine, because he's coming. You don't believe it and Mom doesn't believe it. But he's coming, because he promised. He's probably going to make it a surprise. That's all."

"Well, hello there, almost-birthday girl," Mrs. Gifford said. Cassie loved the way Granny Gifford always seemed so happy to see her.

"It's not for a whole week." She gave the old

woman a big hug. It felt so good to hug someone: it seemed like ages since she and her mom had had a real hug.

"Where's Agatha?"

"Out back somewhere. Up in that tree house, I suppose. Put your things right in her room there, and run tell her we're ready for our tea."

"Agatha?" Cassie called as she went out the back door.

"Up here." Agatha poked her head over the side of the tree house. "Come on up."

"Granny said to tell you that tea's ready."

Agatha's head disappeared. "Want to come have tea with us?"

"Tea?" Cassie heard Jimmy say in disbelief.

"Rose-hip tea, probably," Agatha said. "That's what we usually have. It's Granny's favorite. It's good. Sort of sour-sweet. And we're having chocolate chip cookies today."

"Oh boy!" Jimmy said. "I'll go tell my mom."

Cassie saw Jimmy's feet searching for the first foothold on the tree trunk. Directly above, Agatha waved at her from the top of the ladder.

Agatha looked like she was about to burst as she climbed down. She jumped off the last rung and grabbed Cassie's arm. "Guess what? They're all going to come."

Cassie looked puzzled.

"All the boys. Randy and Bryan and Mike and

Jimmy. All of the ones you invited. Jimmy says they're all going to come to your party."

"Oh," Cassie said. "That's good. Brenda and Stacy will be glad to hear it."

"I think it's going to be a good party," Agatha said. "Don't you? With the space hats and decorations and everything. It won't be an ordinary party. It'll be special, right?"

"I hope so," Cassie said. "I'm sort of worried about the dancing part."

"Well, if you don't want to dance, you don't have to."

The girls had entered the dining room as they talked. Mrs. Gifford was setting the steaming teapot on the table.

"Granny, I invited Jimmy to have some tea with us," Agatha said. "Do we have enough?"

"What we need to ask is do we have enough cookies?" Mrs. Gifford laughed. She picked up the cookie plate and went back toward the kitchen. "Sure, it's all right. Just set out another cup, dear."

Cassie heard the slap of Jimmy's sneakers as he ran across the back porch, and then a knock on the door.

"Come in," she and Agatha called together.

"Hi." Jimmy stopped just inside and smiled shyly.

"Hi." Cassie felt sort of awkward herself. Though they had spent many hours together in the tree house and had often shared Granny Gifford's cookies, Jimmy had rarely been inside the old house.

For a minute the three of them stood looking at one another. Finally Agatha spoke. "Come on in. You sit there." She indicated a chair and sat down in one next to it.

Cassie sat on the other side of Agatha.

"Well, here we are." Mrs. Gifford came back with the plate piled high with fresh chocolate chip cookies. "Plenty of cookies for everyone. Hello there, Jimmy. How are you this afternoon?"

"Fine, thank you."

Mrs. Gifford poured tea into all their cups then put a bit into a saucer to cool for her plant, Roberto. Jimmy watched with interest as she poured the tea from the saucer onto the dirt around the plant, but he didn't say anything. He had already heard from the girls about Roberto's afternoon tea.

Mrs. Gifford stroked the leaves and turned to Jimmy. "Roberto does like his tea, you know."

Jimmy nodded.

Agatha passed the plate of cookies around. Jimmy picked up his cup.

"Sip carefully, Jimmy dear. It's still quite hot," Mrs. Gifford said.

Jimmy sipped. Then his lips puckered slightly and his eyebrows went up. He looked into the cup. He looked up at the three who were watching him and tried to smile. He took another tiny sip and shuddered, pursing his lips and blinking hard.

Agatha and Cassie burst out laughing.

"Girls!" Mrs. Gifford said tersely.

"Well, it's . . . well . . ." Jimmy struggled to find something polite to say about the tea.

"That's perfectly all right, young man," Mrs. Gifford said. "If we all liked the same things it would be a terribly dull world."

"Would you like some milk with your cookies instead?" Agatha got up as she spoke.

"Yes, please," Jimmy said.

"Sometimes we have milk, too." Cassie took another cookie and handed the plate to Jimmy.

"Here you go." Agatha set a glass of milk down in front of him.

"Shall I show Jimmy the pictures of the hats we're going to make?" Cassie asked Agatha.

"Hats?" Jimmy sounded dubious.

"Yes, hats," Agatha said.

"For the party," added Cassie.

"Sure. Let's show him."

"I don't know if Mike or Bryan are going to go for some dumb party hats," Jimmy warned.

"These won't be dumb," Agatha said as Cassie got the magazine.

She took a bite of cookie and flipped through to the right pages. "See, these."

Jimmy nodded noncommittally.

"What do you think?" Agatha asked.

Jimmy shrugged, and Cassie's heart sank. Was this a stupid idea after all?

"No, really," Agatha persisted. "We're going to make all of them kind of like this one." She pointed to the space hat.

"And we'll make all outer-space decorations and stuff," Cassie added. "Like I told you."

"Yeah," Jimmy said, warming up to the idea. "Space hats could be kind of neat. Yeah!"

"Outer-space hats, outer-space decorations, and outer-space music," Mrs. Gifford said.

"Granny, it's not outer-space music!" Agatha said.

"What's not outer-space music?" Jimmy asked.

"Stacy's going to bring her tape player and some of her sister's tapes," Cassie said. "You know, rock music."

"Oh. Is there going to be dancing at this party?"

"Only if you want to," Cassie explained. "Brenda and Stacy want to, but I'm not going to."

"Neither am I!" Jimmy declared. "For sure, I'm not dancing."

"Stacy is going to be very disappointed." Agatha peeked mischievously at Jimmy out of the corner of her eye.

He blushed.

"Well, that's her problem," said Cassie. "Right?"

Jimmy pulled the magazine closer and studied the hats. "You should make this cowboy hat for Angie."

"Then it wouldn't be a space party," Cassie said.

"I know! We could make an outer-space cowboy hat!" Agatha exclaimed excitedly.

A smile slowly spread across Cassie's face. "Yes! And I could make an outer-space princess hat for me."

"Yeah!" Jimmy said, "and an outer-space fireman, and an outer-space nurse, and an . . ."

"Let's do it!" Cassie said. "Let's do it right now!"

"I'll go get the stuff," she called, running off toward Agatha's room. As she picked up the bag, Cassie remembered her mother's words and felt a twinge of guilt. "It'll be fun making the hats together," her mother had said.

Well, too bad. She doesn't really care, Cassie told herself. If she did, she would have stayed home to do it.

Her lips tightened into a straight line as she marched back to the dining room, plunked the bag down on the table, and started pulling out pipe cleaners, foil, and confetti.

Agatha had brought out more glue, tape, and scissors. "We've got some good junk, too. Don't we, Granny?" she said as Mrs. Gifford came back from taking the tea tray into the kitchen. "Can we use that box of old tinsel and things?"

"I think it would be perfect, dear. You know where to find it."

"Wait till you see." Agatha jumped up from the table, ran from the room, and was back in a flash with a box full of old tinsel, pieces of garland, plastic flowers, old Christmas ornaments and parts of ornaments, spools, and other novelties.

Mrs. Gifford brought out some yarn and buttons to add to the collection, and couldn't resist joining the three children at the table.

Mixed Emotions

Late the next morning, Cassie gathered her things together and stuffed them in her overnight case. Mrs. Gifford found a big box and helped the girls put in the hats for Cassie's party. Some of the hats made them laugh all over again.

Cassie was reluctant to leave, but she was also curious to see her mother after her date with that guy. Maybe her mother hadn't liked him and wouldn't want to go on any more dates with him . . . or anybody else.

She picked up the box and Agatha carried the suitcase. Cassie was glad Agatha was going to walk her home—in case her mother was . . . different somehow. "Good-bye, Granny. Thanks for letting me stay over," she said.

"Of course, dear." Mrs. Gifford squeezed Cassie's

shoulders. "You are welcome here anytime. I'd keep you if I could."

"Me too," Agatha agreed, opening the door with her free hand. "I'll be back in a little while, Granny."

"All right. I'll be here."

"Think your mom will like these hats?" Agatha asked.

Cassie nodded. Actually, she was more concerned about how her mother would feel about not getting to help make them. After all, it had been her idea in the first place. Oh well, it was her own fault she wasn't there to help. Cassie wondered just where her mother had gone on her date. Out to dinner and a movie she had said. But what restaurant, what movie?

"I wonder where your mom went last night," Agatha remarked.

Cassie winced. Every once in a while Agatha did that—said exactly what was in Cassie's mind. She shrugged. "Dinner and a movie, she said."

"Do you think she had fun?"

"How do I know?" Cassie muttered. *Fun.* There was that word again. Joel had used it, too. What was so much fun about a date with some dumb guy? And what did Agatha care, anyway?

"I wonder if she'll have another date with him," Agatha went on.

Cassie said nothing. Agatha might know what was on Cassie's mind, but she obviously didn't know how

Cassie felt about it or she wouldn't ask that so cheerfully.

The girls walked in silence, Cassie's thoughts too jumbled for conversation.

She had never been this angry with her mother before, at least not for this long. She got upset about little things that were over quickly, like when her mother wouldn't let her go someplace or scolded her when Cassie felt she didn't deserve it. This time was different, and it didn't feel good. It would be hard to tell anybody, even Agatha.

Maybe especially Agatha. Agatha didn't even have a mother to be angry with. Or a father either, for that matter. Agatha would probably think Cassie was acting like a spoiled brat. She'd probably much rather have her parents divorced and going on dates than have them dead. If it came right down to it, Cassie knew she would, too, but her parents weren't dead, and she didn't see why they had to be divorced either.

She was genuinely sorry about Agatha's parents, but that didn't change her feelings about her own mother's date. Probably the only person who would understand her feelings was her dad. He wouldn't want her mother going out with another man. Sooner or later he'd realize that he belonged with them and he'd come back so they could be a real family again. Why couldn't her mother just wait for him?

Agatha opened the door and Cassie walked into her house, carrying the big box.

"Hi, Cassie," Mrs. Bowen called from the laundry room at the end of the hall.

"Hello," Cassie responded, ducking into her bedroom. She put the box on the floor behind her bed and took the suitcase from Agatha. "Thanks for carrying this."

"Oh, hello there, Agatha. I didn't realize you came in with Cassie." Mrs. Bowen smiled at them from the doorway. "Did you have a good time?"

"Um-hmm," Cassie said, beginning to unpack her suitcase.

"We had lots of fun," Agatha agreed.

"Would you like to have lunch here today, both of you?"

"Sure." Cassie always liked having Agatha eat at her house. So much of the time it was the other way around because of her mother working. And besides, she really wasn't anxious to be alone with her mother.

"I'd like that," said Agatha. "Thank you very much."

"Good. I'll call your grandmother and let her know. In fact, maybe I'll ask her to join us. Joel won't be home. We'll have a ladies-only luncheon. How about that? Then we can get to work on those hats."

Cassie glanced at Agatha and then at the floor. She'd better tell her mother about the hats right now. It served her mother right that they'd done the

92

hats without her, but what was Agatha going to think?

Her mother was all the way down the hall when Cassie stuck her head out the door. "We already made the hats."

Mrs. Bowen turned around in surprise. "You did?"

"Yeah, Jimmy and Agatha and I. We just . . . well, I showed them the pictures and then we just got all excited, so we started making them. Granny Gifford helped, too."

"Oh." Mrs. Bowen smiled halfheartedly. Cassie wanted to crawl under the rug. "Well, I guess the important thing is that they got done, right?"

"Right," said Cassie. She went back into her room. Her eyes met Agatha's briefly, which only made her feel guiltier than ever. She sat on the edge of her bed and gave the box a little kick.

"Your mom was planning on helping you make the hats?" Agatha's remark was half statement, half question.

Cassie nodded.

"Why didn't you tell us? We could have waited."

"I didn't want to wait," Cassie said crossly. "It's all right. She doesn't really care."

"Well, we still have to make the decorations. She could help us with that," Agatha suggested.

Cassie nodded. "Let's go out front. I don't feel like being in the house." She led the way to the front step, where the two girls sat down side by side. Cassie glanced up the street. The mail truck wasn't in sight.

She stretched her legs out in front of her, noticing that her jeans were getting a little short. She'd be needing bigger ones soon. Especially with winter coming. The September air had an autumn crispness to it, and the warm sun felt good.

"I hope it's like this for my picnic next week." Cassie leaned back on her elbows.

Agatha stretched out, too. "So do I."

The warm sun, combined with the fact that they had stayed up late reading and talking and planning Cassie's birthday, made both girls sleepy. Cassie closed her eyes.

She felt herself sort of drifting, just on the edge of sleep, when she heard a familiar sound off in the distance. A motor revved, then slowed. Brakes squeaked, then the motor revved again. Cassie lay listening to the pattern of sound getting louder.

She pictured the mail truck making its way down the street, squeaking to a stop in front of each mailbox. She tried to pinpoint just where it was as the sound came closer. Now it must be on the next block. Now it must be crossing the street to the house on the corner of her block. That meant just four more houses. *Vroom, squeak, cha-clunk.* Now three houses.

Another sound. Footsteps. A woman's heels, clicking down the street. From the edge of sleep, Cassie listened. *Vroom, squeak, cha-clunk.* Two more houses. *Click-click, click-click.*

"Well, if you two don't pick the craziest places to take a nap! I wouldn't think you'd be very comfortable there!"

Cassie opened her eyes. Mrs. Gifford was smiling down at them.

"The sun feels good, Granny," said Agatha, squinting.

"I'll bet it does at that. It's a lovely day. I'm so pleased that your mother invited me to lunch, Cassie dear. Is she inside?"

"I'll tell her you're here." Cassie got up and glanced over her shoulder. The mail truck had stopped in front of her house.

"I'll get the mail," Agatha offered.

"Mom, Granny Gifford's here."

"Oh, good! Tell her to come on in the kitchen."

"She says to go on in the kitchen," Cassie said, stepping out of the way and holding the door open.

Mrs. Bowen came through the kitchen door, wiping her hands on a towel. "Hello, Amanda. I'm glad you could come on such short notice. Come on in while I finish up."

"Lunch will be ready in a few minutes, Cassie," her mother said as Cassie backed out the front door.

Agatha was pulling the mail out of the box as Cassie leaped down the steps.

"Is it there?" Cassie asked.

Agatha held the mail out to her. "I haven't looked."

Cassie took the stack in both hands. "There's a lot today," she said. She sat down on the steps and put the pile in her lap. Please, let it be here today, she thought. Please, please, please! She picked up each piece and sorted it beside her on the step. Two sale catalogs, four advertisements, five letters for her mom, even one for Joel. Nothing for her.

Agatha put an arm around her friend. "There are still six more days," she reminded her.

Cassie nodded and counted on her fingers. "Six days to get mail and seven until my real birthday."

"Right."

"It's my real birthday that's the most important thing."

"I know."

"Lunch is ready, girls," Mrs. Bowen called.

Cassie picked up the mail, and the two of them walked into the house.

"Well, that's wonderful, Jean. I think it's nice that you're seeing a young man," Mrs. Gifford was saying when the girls went in to take their seats at the table. "I've had many lonely years since Frank died. Of course, it's much better now that Agatha has come to live with me." She smiled and patted her granddaughter's hand.

"Mom doesn't have to be lonely," I said. "She has me and Joel."

"And she's lucky to have you," Mrs. Gifford said.

"You're a treasure for sure, and your brother too, no doubt. But you'll both be growing up before you know it. Your mama needs grown-up friends as well."

"I'll be Mom's friend even when I'm grown-up, and Agatha will be yours, too. Won't you, Agatha?"

Agatha nodded.

"We'll fix lunch and invite both of you over, and we'll all be together just like today," Cassie went on.

"We'll be delighted to come," Mrs. Gifford said. "I'm sure your luncheons will be just as lovely as this one."

When the Giffords left, Cassie went out into the backyard. She wandered around, poking at the ground with the toes of her sneakers. She plucked a leaf off a bush, tore it into little bits, and studied all the pieces in the palm of her hand. She gave a quick blow, and the bits of leaf scattered, except for one that stuck to her palm. She blew again. She turned her hand over and shook it. Still the tiny piece of leaf stuck. Cassie picked it off with her thumb and finger and flicked it away. "I guess you don't know when you aren't wanted," she said, brushing her hands together.

She picked up a twig and snapped it in two and then snapped each half again. She tossed the pieces in the air, and swung at them.

She sat on the back step and leaned her chin in

her hands. The little village she had made in the flower garden last weekend with twigs and leaves and dirt and a couple of old bottle caps was mostly still there. It was actually more like a campground than a village.

Cassie squatted down beside it to fix a broken place in the tiny fence. She smoothed the stream and made it a little longer. She looked around for something to make another bridge and found an almost perfect piece of bark. It was just a little too short. Cassie tried to make the stream narrower to fit the bridge, but she bumped one of her tents with her knee. Trying to set the tent back up she knocked over a tree.

She let out an exasperated sigh and stood up. If only she could think of something to do. She could be making the hats with her mother if she hadn't already done it with Agatha and Jimmy and Granny Gifford. With another sigh she walked up the steps and opened the door.

Just at that moment, the phone rang. Her hopes rising, Cassie ran to pick up the receiver. "Hello," she said.

"Hello," said a man's voice. "May I please speak with your mother?"

"I'll get her," Cassie replied. She looked quizzically at the receiver as she set it down. She had been hoping it would be Agatha, maybe even her father. "Mom, telephone."

"Thanks, honey." Her mother put a load of clean laundry on the table and picked up the phone. "Hello? Oh, hello."

By the way her mother's voice changed on the second *hello*, Cassie could tell it wasn't some salesman on the phone. She had a good guess who it might be. Eavesdropping wasn't allowed, but her mother would probably appreciate some help folding the laundry. Cassie picked up one of her shirts and smoothed out the wrinkles.

"Yes, thank you. Yes, I did too, very much."

Disgusting. Her mother was smiling at the stupid telephone. Suddenly Cassie didn't want to hear any more. She went into the living room and turned on the television set, loud. But she could still hear her mother talking and laughing on the phone. Cassie pressed pillows against her ears and stared at the TV picture, trying to figure out what was going on.

After a while her mother came in and turned the set down. She was smiling. Not at Cassie, just to herself. Cassie went to the kitchen and dialed Agatha's number. "Hi, Agatha. It's me."

"Hi. What's up?"

"Want to go over to Stacy's and learn how to dance? She said we could come watch 'StarDancers' on TV today. Remember?"

"Yes, but I thought you didn't want to dance."

"Just because I learn how, doesn't mean I have to do it at my party, does it? Do you want to go or not?"

"All right. Let me ask Granny. Hold on."

Cassie twisted the phone cord around her finger and looked at the clock. That show started at 3:30. She knew because sometimes Joel turned it on and danced, but only when he didn't know anyone was watching. Cassie thought he looked pretty silly. Especially when he pretended he was dancing with somebody.

"I can go," Agatha said.

"Good. I'll call Stacy and tell her we're coming; then I'll meet you on the corner."

"Okay. See you."

"Okay. Bye." Cassie hung up the phone and started dialing Stacy's number.

"Agatha and I are going over to Stacy's for a while. Okay, Mom?" she called out as she dialed.

Mrs. Bowen came into the kitchen. "How long are you going to be gone?"

"I'll be home by five-thirty. Oh, hi. May I please speak to Stacy?"

"What are you going to do over there?"

"We're going to watch that dance show so we can all learn how to dance for my party. Yes, oh hi, Stacy. It's me, Cassie. Do you still want us to come over? . . . All right . . . Yes, Agatha too."

"Cassie, wait a minute," Mrs. Bowen said.

"Just a minute, Stacy. Please, Mom. This is very important."

"I thought you'd be home all afternoon. I was sort of hoping . . ."

"We planned this, Mom, but I forgot. Please, can I go?"

Her mother hesitated.

"I know. I know it's almost starting," Cassie said into the phone. "Just one minute, okay?" She looked anxiously at her mother.

"All right. You may go," Mrs. Bowen said.

"Okay, Mom. Thanks. Stacy? . . . We'll be right there, okay? Okay, see you. Bye."

"Bye, Mom." Cassie was out the door in a flash. Agatha was already waiting on the corner, and the two of them ran most of the three blocks to Stacy's house.

Surprise Visit

On Sunday afternoon Joel was out mowing lawns for the Petersons and the Becks. Cassie tiptoed into his room to check out his portable tape player. He'd kill her if he ever found her touching it. She touched it anyway. It was almost like Stacy's sister's. It would be easy to work. Too bad her brother wasn't as nice as Stacy's sister.

Cassie looked through his box of tapes. She picked out one by a group she recognized from the "Star-Dancers" show. She took it and the tape player and tiptoed into her own room and closed the door.

Cassie set the machine on her desk, put in the tape, and pushed the play button. Yipes! Too loud! She turned it off quickly and listened for footsteps. To her relief, she heard nothing.

She found the volume control, turned it in a direction she hoped was down, and pushed play again. The tape went around, but there was no sound at all. Cassie slowly turned up the volume until she could hear it.

Her head nodded to the beat. How did that tricky step go? Agatha had caught on really fast. Cassie was the only one of the four who couldn't seem to manage it. At Stacy's she had pretended she didn't care.

Really, she didn't care. Except that it would be pretty embarrassing to be the only one at her own party who didn't know how to dance. Not that she planned on dancing.

She did a couple of easy steps that she had learned. Maybe the tricky one was cross front, point, cross front. No, that still took her the wrong direction.

She waited for the next song and picked up the beat. She bobbed her head, snapped her fingers, then started moving her feet. Side, cross back, cross front, point and step. That was it! Don't cross after the point! Okay.

"I can do it!" she said out loud. She repeated the step a few more times. "So *who* doesn't know how to dance?" She gave herself a mocking grin in the mirror.

A knock on her door startled her. Cassie pushed the off button and stood with her elbows out, back against the tape player. "Who is it?"

"It's me." Her mother opened the door. "Did I hear music in here?"

Cassie nodded.

"What was it coming from?"

Reluctantly Cassie stepped aside so her mother could see Joel's tape player.

"Did you ask him?"

Cassie shook her head and looked at the floor.

"Don't you think that would have been a good idea?"

"Yes," she said in a barely audible voice.

"Well, that's not what I came in here about. I want you to come and meet someone. Put that back in Joel's room and come into the living room."

Cassie breathed a sigh of relief. She had expected to get in a lot more trouble than that for using something of her brother's without permission. She still could, if Joel ever found out. Quickly, she returned it to his room and went into the living room.

A man was sitting on the sofa. He looked like the guys in the aspirin commercials on television. He stood up and smiled at Cassie as she came into the room. Her stomach flopped. She wanted to turn around and go right back to her room, but she didn't dare.

"Lyle, this is Cassie. Cassie this is my friend, Lyle Kester."

Mr. Kester held out his hand. "Hello, Cassie. I've

been looking forward to meeting you." He spoke pleasantly. He was tall, with brown hair that was getting thin on top, and a sort of pointy chin. Not gross, but not as handsome as her father, who had a nice broad chin and lots of curly hair.

Reluctantly, Cassie shook his hand. "Hi."

"Sit down, sweetie," Mrs. Bowen said, "and visit with us a few minutes. Lyle just stopped by for a little while."

Cassie sat in the rocking chair. Lyle and her mother sat back down on the sofa. Cassie noticed that her mother had on her favorite peach sweater and her brown slacks. She didn't usually dress like that around home. So her mother had been expecting this little visit!

"You must be in about what . . . fourth grade?" Mr. Kester said. He was still smiling; his teeth lined up like little white soldiers.

"Fifth."

"Cassie enjoys school, don't you, sweetie?"

What a dopey thing to say, Cassie thought, wishing her mother would wipe that gushy smile off her face.

Cassie was the only one not smiling. She felt all hot inside. Hot and angry. Her mother should have told her he was coming over here. She should have told her he was the one her mother wanted her to meet.

"I'll bet she's a good student," Mr. Kester said. His smile was shrinking and he squeezed his knees nervously. Cassie thought the conversation was getting dopier by the minute.

"Cassie, would you like to get us all some lemonade? There's a full pitcher in the refrigerator."

She was glad to leave the room. She took three glasses out of the cupboard and banged them down on the counter. Joel came in the back door just as she slammed the freezer door shut. He watched as she plunked ice cubes into each glass and shoved the ice container back in the freezer.

"What's with you?"

"Nothing," she snapped, taking the pitcher of lemonade from the refrigerator.

"Little stormy in here if you ask me."

"Nobody asked you."

"Who's the lemonade for?"

"Mom and *her friend* and me. If you want some, get your own."

"Her friend? Lyle? Lyle's here? Oh, wow. I want to ask him about that story he wrote." Joel hurried into the living room.

Cassie stared after him. What a traitor! Just because this creepy guy wrote science fiction, Joel thought he was Mr. Wonderful. Cassie knew who the real Mr. Wonderful was. She wasn't going to forget as easily as Joel and her mother had.

She put the glasses on a tray and went into the living room.

"Didn't you bring some lemonade for your brother?" her mother asked.

"I didn't know he wanted any," Cassie said. She picked up her own glass and sat down in the chair farthest away from everyone else.

"That's okay. She'd probably put poison in it," Joel said with a laugh.

Not a bad idea, Cassie thought.

"I can't believe she'd even think of something like that," Mr. Kester said, smiling at Cassie again.

Cassie didn't smile back. You'd be surprised what I might think, she thought to herself. Your drink is the one I'd like to put poison in. And maybe tacks under your tires so they'd all go flat. No, then he'd just have to hang around while they got fixed. Bad idea.

Mr. Kester seemed relieved when Joel turned the conversation back to science fiction. Cassie pretended to listen for a while. Then she stopped pretending.

She just watched what was happening in her own living room. Her brother was asking question after question, encouraging Lyle Kester to go on about his stupid science fiction. And her mother, grinning and nodding and sipping her lemonade, was obviously delighted that they were getting along so well. The whole thing made Cassie sick. Joel and her mother were both acting like that man was a king or something. The whole thing was just stupid. It made her want to vomit.

Cassie stood up. "I think I have some homework to do," she said. "I'd better go get started."

"I have to be going soon, too," Mr. Kester said.

"It was nice meeting you, Cassie. Maybe next time we'll talk about something more interesting to you than science fiction." He smiled at her with a hopeful expression.

Cassie nodded. "Good-bye." She walked quickly out of the room. "Maybe next time there won't be a next time," she muttered on her way down the hall.

Emergency!

The week was a long one for Cassie. At school, recesses were fun because all the girls who were invited wanted to play with her and talk about her party. Some girls who weren't invited got their feelings hurt. Cassie felt bad about that, but she tried to explain that it had to be a small party.

The last part of each day, during science, Cassie would watch the clock. It wasn't that she minded science, it was just that she knew the mail would be waiting in the box at home and a letter might be there.

As soon as the bell rang, she would rush out the door, hurrying Agatha along. Agatha soon gave up trying to talk—

But the letter didn't come. Not on Monday or Tuesday or Wednesday. Cassie knew that Agatha wanted her to get that letter almost as much as she wanted it herself, so neither girl ever said anything about it. They'd just put the mail in the house and go over to the Giffords'.

Even playing at Granny's wasn't as much fun as usual. Agatha would suggest a game and Cassie would start in, but pretty soon she'd be thinking about her father again. Would he write or just surprise her? A surprise would be nice, but it would be better to know for sure. Not that *she* wasn't sure, but it would be good to have the letter to prove it to her brother and her mom. And it was hard to wait.

Then Cassie would realize that she'd forgotten it was her turn and Agatha would say, "It's all right. Let's not play this anymore today. I think I'll read."

So they'd both get books and find a cozy spot in the tree house or in Agatha's room. Agatha would soon be engrossed, but Cassie would read a sentence or two, the words would stop making sense, and she'd be thinking again.

She'd imagine him walking in the door, right in the middle of her birthday party maybe, thinking he was going to surprise her. But he'd be surprised, too, seeing his little girl having a party with dancing and rock music and everything.

Then Sunday they'd go to the lake. She'd challenge him to a race and beat him to the water. He'd still beat her swimming to the buoy, though.

Joel and her mother would have to admit they'd been wrong all along.

Thinking about her mother made Cassie feel lonely in a strange new way. She'd always been able to go to her mom when she felt hurt or confused or sad, especially during this past year. Even before, her dad was more available for good times, when he wanted to be, while her mom always seemed to be there with the hugs and the right words when Cassie needed them.

Not since her mother started seeing that Mr. Lyle Kester, though. That changed everything. Cassie definitely didn't want to think about that. With a sigh, she'd try again to read her book, but it wasn't any use.

Later, at home, it felt weird too. Her mom was always watching her and trying to make ordinary conversation. But Cassie didn't feel like talking.

On Wednesday night it was Cassie's turn to clean up after dinner. She planned on going to her room afterward in spite of the fact that her favorite TV show, about a pretty normal but slightly crazy family, was on. Usually the three of them watched it together.

Joel had already turned it on and was sitting in the chair. Her mom was on the sofa. They were laughing at the show as Cassie walked through, so she stopped to check it out, just for a minute. Her mom turned and patted the spot next to her on the sofa.

Cassie hesitated. The show was funny and she hated to miss it. The father was always trying to help his kids but usually ended up in trouble himself. Cassie walked over and sat down close to the spot her mother had patted—but not too close.

After a while Mrs. Bowen reached over and put a hand on Cassie's shoulder. It felt good. Cassie lay down with her head in her mother's lap, and her mom smoothed her hair. When they laughed, Cassie felt her mother's lap wiggle. It made her laugh harder.

During the commercial Joel went to the kitchen for some chips. He passed her the bag.

"Thanks." She took a handful, amazed that she hadn't had to ask.

"Don't mention it, kid. I'm a nice guy, you know."

"Huh!" Cassie scoffed, but she smiled at him. The icy feeling inside of her seemed to be melting away. It felt good to be with her family, laughing and watching TV and munching chips. Only her dad was missing, and he'd be there in just a few days.

The warm feeling stayed with Cassie the next day. She didn't have quite so much trouble paying attention, even during science. And when she checked the mail and there was no letter, she still felt confident her dad was going to surprise her.

Cassie made spaghetti for dinner that night, and her mom said it was the best she'd ever had. Even Joel praised it.

As soon as dinner was over, Mrs. Bowen reminded her children that she was going to a peace group meeting. "I've got to hurry. My ride will be here in about two minutes."

It was Joel's turn to clean up, so Cassie wandered into the living room. She had hoped that they could all watch television together again. Still, she was glad that her mom was going to the peace group, not doing something else.

As Cassie picked up the TV schedule and checked out the programs, a car pulled into the driveway. "Mom," she called, "Carol's here." Carol and her mom took turns driving each other to the meetings.

Mrs. Bowen looked in from the kitchen anxiously. "Cassie, it's not . . ." she began, but was interrupted by the doorbell.

"I'll get it." Cassie bounced to the door. "Hi Carol—" Her voice fell as she found herself looking up at Lyle Kester.

"Not this time," Mr. Kester teased.

Cassie froze in the doorway.

Mr. Kester gave a sort of nervous chuckle. "I believe your mother is expecting me to take her to a meeting tonight. May I come in?"

Cassie backed up without a word. She looked around, but her mother had disappeared.

"Going to watch some TV tonight?" Mr. Kester asked.

Cassie still had the TV schedule in her hand. She shrugged.

"What's your favorite?"

" 'StarDancers,' " Cassie lied. She didn't want to tell this intruder her true favorite program. It was none of his business.

"I like the show that's on on Wednesday nights," Mr. Kester said. "What's the name? The one with the funny kids." He chuckled again nervously.

Cassie gave him a quick look. Did Lyle Kester really like that show or had he just guessed it was her favorite? Probably he was just trying to make her think he was a nice guy. No way. A creep is a creep no matter what shows he happens to watch.

Mr. Kester glanced around the room anxiously. Cassie plopped down in the rocking chair and pretended to study the TV schedule.

Joel came in from the kitchen, wiping his hands on his pants. "Hi, Lyle. Good to see you."

"Good to see you, too. How's it going?" Mr. Kester smiled and extended a hand.

Joel offered his own still-damp hand. "Dishes," he said with a shrug.

"I do that job myself," Mr. Kester said with another little chuckle.

This guy's a laugh a minute, Cassie chided silently.

Mrs. Bowen came in carrying her coat and purse. "Hi, Lyle. Sorry to keep you waiting."

Cassie noticed that her mother had combed her hair and put on fresh lipstick. I wish she'd keep him waiting so long he'd go away and never come back, she thought.

"No problem," Mr. Kester said pleasantly.

No problem! That's what he thinks! Easy for him to be all nice talk and smiles!

"Well, we'd better go or we'll be late," Mrs. Bowen said. Mr. Kester stepped around and helped her with her coat.

Leave her alone, you jerk! She can put on her own coat! Cassie wanted to scream, but she kept her mouth shut and looked at the TV schedule.

Mrs. Bowen kissed Joel good-bye and walked over to her daughter. Cassie offered her cheek but didn't return the kiss. Her mother patted her on the knee.

"Remember, you both have school tomorrow. I expect you to get yourselves to bed on time, and be sure to lock the door. I left the number by the phone in case of emergency. Okay? Bye-bye now."

"Good night," Mr. Kester said with a wave. "Nice to see you again."

"So long," said Joel.

"Bye," Cassie muttered. She tossed the TV schedule on the floor.

"It's just a peace group meeting," Joel said, flipping on the television. "No big deal."

"If it's no big deal, why doesn't she just ride with Carol like she usually does?" Cassie retorted. "Anyway, who says I care?"

Joel picked the schedule up off the floor and

thumbed through it. "Lyle's not such a bad guy, you know."

"If you like creeps," Cassie muttered.

"What?" Joel asked as he switched channels.

"Nothing." Cassie got up and stomped off to her room. "Nothing, except my mother is acting dopey over some creep," she said, leaning against her door. "She's acting as bad as Stacy.

"Emergency! Emergency! A grown-up woman has boy-crazyitis! Send in the doctors! Send in the men with the straitjackets!" Cassie raged, pacing back and forth in her room. "Cure this woman quick before she ruins her daughter's life forever!"

She kicked the leg of her chair. It hurt her toes. "So who cares?" she said, flopping down on her bed. "Who cares, PeeWee? Who cares if I hurt myself? Who cares if I'm going to be ten years old in just three days? Who cares if my birthday party is a big flop? Let her go to her old peace group meeting with Mr. Lyle Kester."

Suddenly, Cassie was crying. She hadn't meant to cry, but the tears were hot on her cheeks and her body shook with sobs. She leaned over and buried her face in her pillow.

"Oh, please! Oh, please!" she wailed. She didn't know "oh please" what, exactly. "Oh, please, don't let this be happening," maybe. Or, "Oh, please, let Daddy come back and make everything all right," or even "Oh, please, don't make me grow up!"

She buried her face in the bedclothes, trying to muffle the sound of her crying, but the sobs and the wails kept coming. "Oh, please! Oh, please!"

Cassie felt a hand on her shoulder and looked up to see Joel. She hadn't heard him come in. "Go away," she said, hiding her face again.

But Joel didn't go. He sat on the edge of her bed and rubbed her back, just the way her mother often did. Cassie didn't give any sign of responding, but secretly she was glad he hadn't gone away. It felt nice, being comforted by her brother. Not so alone.

"Listen, Cass," Joel said after a while. "Try not to be upset about Mom seeing Lyle. I mean, it's not like she's going to run off with him or anything."

Cassie stiffened.

"It's just, well, she gets lonely. I mean, we're lucky it's Lyle and not some real jerk. Like the guy Danny's mom is going with. Danny says he hits her all the time."

Cassie looked up at him.

"I'm not kidding. Last week Danny had this big bruise on his cheek where the guy hit him when he tried to stop the creep from hitting his mother.

"And Janice's mother is living with some guy who just watches TV and drinks beer all the time. He talks to her mom but he never says a word to her or her little brother. She says it's awful."

"Who's Janice?" Cassie asked.

Joel looked away. "Just this girl at school." He

said it with a shrug, but Cassie didn't miss the blush.

"You like her, huh? Did you dance with her at the dance you went to last week?"

Joel grinned. "Yeah. Hey, listen. Mom said you wanted to have some music and dancing at your party on Saturday. Do you want to borrow my tape player and some tapes?"

Cassie looked at him in disbelief. "You mean it?"

"Sure I mean it. I mean, I'd want you to be careful and not let anybody else fool around and mess it up or anything."

"I wouldn't," Cassie said. "I mean, I would—not mess it up or anything." She was amazed that her brother would be so nice to her. "I'd take care of it myself and not let anybody else even touch it."

"All right then," Joel said. He stood up. "Come on. Let's go pick out some good tapes."

Cassie grabbed a tissue from the box on her desk and followed her brother. It felt strange to be invited into his room. It felt strange to stand there next to him, watching him sort through tapes . . . for her. When they were both much younger, they used to play together sometimes, but that was a long time ago. She couldn't even remember the last time the two of them had done something.

But here he was offering to let her use his tape player and choosing tapes for her party. Hard to believe.

"Here's a good one," he said, slipping a tape into

the cassette player. He pushed the button and bobbed his head to the beat of the song.

Cassie watched his face until Joel seemed to sense her eyes on him. He looked at her. She glanced away, half expecting to hear him say, "What are you staring at?"

Instead he said, "Can you dance?"

"A little," Cassie said.

"Come on. I'll show you some stuff."

He picked up the cassette player and went into the living room. "More space in here," he said, moving the rocking chair back. "Now watch this." He stepped from side to side and did the circle-and-arm-lift movement Cassie had learned from Stacy.

She did it, too.

Joel was impressed. "Hey, all right! Try this one." He did the tricky cross back–cross front step.

Cassie took a deep breath and tried it. "Oooops! I keep getting mixed up on that one," she said.

"You just cross before you should. Just step down after you do the touch."

"After the point, you mean?" Cassie asked. "I keep forgetting that."

"Instead of just pointing, think of it as a little kick. That's what I do. Like this." Joel did the step.

Cassie walked through it.

"Right. Now faster."

Beaming, Cassie kept up with him.

"Now try this." Joel seemed to be doing the same

steps, but instead of going from side to side, he was moving around in a square.

Cassie shook her head.

"It's not hard. Just kick and step to the front, see? Yeah, only when you step, you pivot, okay? Yeah, that's it."

"I'm doing it!" Cassie exclaimed.

They danced through three more songs.

"You're pretty good, for a kid," Joel said when the tape ended. "Whew! I'm getting thirsty!"

"I'll get us some orange juice," Cassie offered.

As soon as they finished the juice, Joel put on another tape and they started dancing again. He changed his arm movement, alternating one arm in front and one in back as he snapped his fingers.

Cassie picked it right up, grinning at her brother.

He showed her a couple more new steps, slowing them down until she caught on and not teasing her at all when she had trouble. Cassie was having so much fun, she was surprised when Joel clapped his hand to his head and yelled, "Jeez!"

"What?"

"Look at the time!" Joel scooped up the cassette player and a handful of tapes. "It's after nine! Mom will be home any minute! I've still got homework to do, and you're supposed to be in bed!"

Cassie looked. He was right. Where had the time gone? She grabbed the glasses they'd used and ran them to the kitchen. Joel deposited his stuff in his room and came back to put the rocking chair in place.

Then they both ran around the house turning off most of the lights and making sure everything was as it should be. As they went into their own rooms, Cassie stopped at her door. "Joel," she said. "Thanks."

Joel nodded and almost smiled. "Sure. Good night, kid."

"Good night."

Cassie jumped out of her clothes and into her nightgown. She climbed into bed and had barely made herself comfortable when she heard the car pull up outside.

Then she remembered Lyle. What if he came inside with her mother and they sat talking in the living room or something? She strained to hear, but on second thought decided she didn't want to hear, so she covered her ears with her pillow. She couldn't contain her curiosity, though, and lifted the pillow in time to hear the front door close.

She heard no voices—only footsteps, her mom's footsteps, coming down the hall. Cassie tucked the pillow under her head and closed her eyes, pretending to be asleep. The footsteps paused at her door, then again at Joel's.

"Everything all right?" she heard her mother ask.

"Fine, Mom," Joel answered. "Did you have a good meeting?"

"Yes, it was a good discussion, but I'm tired. Are you doing homework?"

"I'm almost done."

"Good. You should get to sleep."

"I will. Good night, Mom."

"Good night, son."

Cassie heard her mother go on into her own room and come out a minute later to go into the bathroom. The next thing she heard was her mom calling her to get up for school.

Party Time!

After school, Cassie and Agatha hurried to Cassie's house. Cassie checked the mail as usual, and this time she found two envelopes with her name on them.

"Oh!" Agatha's face lit up. "Did you get it?"

Cassie's hands trembled slightly as she studied the two envelopes. "This one is from my Aunt Joyce," she said. "I recognize the handwriting because she always writes to Mom. This other one could be it. See, it's from California and that's where Daddy is. It's sort of like his handwriting, but I'm not sure."

She took in a big gulp of air and handed the mystery envelope to Agatha. "Here. You hold it a minute. I'm going to save it for last." Cassie ripped open the first envelope. Sure enough, it was from her aunt, uncle, and cousin Lisa. Lisa had drawn a funny cat inside the card. Cassie showed it to Agatha, and gingerly took the other envelope.

It had a return address but not a name. That might be her dad's handwriting. It was cursive, and usually he printed, but his cursive could look like that. It was from the right state, anyway. Cassie turned the envelope over in her hands.

Agatha watched. "Do you think that's it?"

Cassie turned the envelope over one more time before she opened it and pulled out the card. *To Our Darling Granddaughter,* it said. Of course. It was from Grandma and Grandpa Bowen. They lived in California and sent her a card every year. It always had money inside.

She had seen them only a few times. Grandma always smelled like some kind of flowers and wanted to hug her all the time. Grandpa had tweaked her nose each time he'd seen her but never had much to say. They were nice but far away.

Cassie sighed. She didn't know whether she felt disappointed or relieved. A card this late might say her father wasn't coming.

"Well?" Agatha said finally.

Cassie pushed the card back into the envelope. "It's not from my dad. It's from my grandma and grandpa. They live in California, too."

"Well, it's good you got birthday cards," Agatha said hesitantly. "Anyway, there's still tomorrow."

"Right," said Cassie. "Come on. Let's get the stuff to make the decorations."

The decorations came out great. Spaceships and planets and galaxies. Mrs. Bowen admired them over and over as she helped Cassie and Agatha hang them from the ceiling and walls on Saturday morning.

Even Joel thought they looked neat. He helped move the furniture to make room for dancing, and he set up his cassette player and tapes. "Remember," he warned, "don't let anybody fool around with this."

"I won't," Cassie assured him.

Joel smiled at her. "I know. Otherwise I wouldn't let you touch it."

"Your brother's being nice," Agatha observed when Joel was out of the room.

Cassie nodded. "I told you birthdays are special in our house. Even yucky brothers are nice to you." She laughed.

When the living room was decorated, the girls went into the kitchen to start on the cupcakes Cassie's mom had baked. Mrs. Bowen helped them turn each cupcake into a little spaceship with frosting and colored candy beads.

Joel came in with the mail, and Cassie looked up anxiously. "Anything for me?"

"Not unless you want the bills and junk mail." Her brother hit her playfully over the head with the stack of envelopes.

Cassie ducked, then went back to her task, blinking as she concentrated on finishing the last cupcake.

As she set it on the plate she avoided meeting any-one's eyes and resolutely announced, "We'd better get ready now."

In Cassie's room, the girls changed into their clothes for the party. "I'm sorry you didn't get the letter," Agatha said.

"Well, I didn't get one saying he's *not* coming," Cassie said sharply. "He could still call. Anyway, my real birthday isn't until tomorrow. He'll probably just walk right in and surprise me." She was quiet as she selected a hair ribbon from the bureau. "I hope everybody likes the hats we made for them. Do you think they will?"

"Sure," Agatha said. "They're great hats. They're works of art." She grinned at Cassie.

"Oh, my hair's being so weird. Look! It sticks out over here." Cassie tried to tie her hair back with the ribbon, but the short ends popped out in front of her ears.

"Put some water on it," Agatha suggested. "Come on, I'll do it for you." She pulled Cassie into the bath-room.

"I wish I hadn't invited boys. They'll probably hate this party. I think I hate this party."

"Nobody's going to hate this party. It's going to be fun. Let's go put our hats on."

"Cassie," Mrs. Bowen called, "someone's at the door."

Cassie sighed and looked at Agatha. "Well, here

goes. Who do you think will be the first one? Besides us, I mean."

"Stacy," Agatha said.

"Right," Cassie said, opening the door to face Jimmy and Mike.

Jimmy grinned at her. "Hi," he said nervously, handing her a present. "This is for you."

"Thanks," Cassie said. "Come on in."

Mike followed Jimmy into the living room, handing Cassie a package as he walked past her.

"Thank you," said Cassie. She put the gifts on the coffee table.

Jimmy and Mike looked at each other. Cassie and Agatha looked at each other, then at Jimmy and Mike. Cassie laughed nervously.

"So, are we the first ones here?" Jimmy asked.

"Yes," said Cassie. "Except for Agatha, but she's been here all morning, helping with the decorations and stuff."

Jimmy scanned the room. "They're neat," he said.

"We were just about to put our hats on," Agatha said, going over to the cardboard box. It was decorated, too.

"There's a special hat for everybody," Cassie explained.

"I know," Jimmy said. "I helped make them, remember?"

"I remember." Cassie handed him his hat.

"I made yours," Agatha said, handing Mike one

with glittered lightning bolts and long purple antennae. She smiled shyly.

Mike turned it around in his hands. "What's it supposed to be?"

"They're space hats," Jimmy said. "Can't you tell?" He put his on his head. It was green and had egg carton cups covered with orange glitter glued all over it. "How's this look?"

"Weird!" Mike said. He held his hat in his hand.

Cassie put on a hat with blue streamers and gold antennae. "I'm a space princess," she said.

Mike looked at Agatha. Her hat had lightning bolts too, smaller ones, and musical notes hanging from the sides. "What are you supposed to be?"

Agatha blushed. "I'm a space rock star. Yours is a rock star, too, but you're a drummer and I'm a singer."

The doorbell rang. "It's Stacy and Brenda," Cassie announced, opening the door for them to come in. "And here's Angie and Rachel and Kristi, too."

The girls filed in and put their gifts on the table.

"Cheryl can't come," Kristi said. "Her dad said she's sick."

"Hi, everybody," Stacy called, flashing Jimmy a big smile.

Cassie tried to catch Agatha's eye, but she was looking at Mike.

"So what's all this?" Brenda asked, pointing to the hats.

"These are our space hats," Cassie said. "I'll get yours."

"Pretty weird," Brenda said. "What kind of hat is this supposed to be?"

"Yours is a space doctor," Cassie explained, passing out hats to the others. "And Angie and Rachel are space cowgirls. I'm a space princess."

"Why didn't you make me a space princess, too?" Brenda asked.

Cassie shrugged. "Well, I . . . well, you used to say you wanted to be a doctor. I didn't know what to make Stacy's, so I made hers a nurse so it would go with yours."

"Oh," said Brenda. She didn't seem to be very impressed.

The doorbell rang again. This time it was Randy and Bryan.

"Well, that's everybody," Cassie announced as she followed them to where the others were standing around.

Brenda had put her hat back in the box. She watched Randy add his package to the pile on the table.

"Hey! Cool hats!" he said. "Where's mine?" He spied the box and headed for it.

Cassie handed him a hat covered with red tinsel. "It's a fireman's hat, and these are the flashing lights," she explained, indicating a row of gold spools across the front.

"Oh, wow! A fireman from outer space!" He put it on and began to whoop and wail like a fire engine.

Brenda went over and took her hat back out of the box. "I'm an outer-space doctor," she said to Randy.

"Yeah, cool! These are really neat! Who made them? Did you?" Randy asked, turning to Cassie.

Cassie nodded, giving the last hat to Bryan. "Me and Agatha and Jimmy."

"Cool decorations too." Randy gave a hanging balloon ship a bop.

"Why don't we have some music now," Stacy said, "so we can start dancing and stuff?" She looked at Jimmy, who immediately sat down on the sofa.

Cassie selected a tape to put in the cassette player.

Stacy came up beside her. "What tapes have you got? I brought some of my sister's, in case we need them."

"My brother's got good tapes, too," Cassie said.

"What are you playing?" Stacy grabbed Cassie's hand and read the label. "That's a good one. Go ahead and play that one first. We can play some of these later. She put her purse on the bookshelf beside the cassette player.

Cassie pushed the play button and the music started.

All the kids stood around looking at each other, or trying not to look at each other.

"Well, isn't anybody going to dance?" Stacy asked,

gazing hopefully at Jimmy. He turned and started talking to Mike.

"Come on, Brenda," Stacy said in exasperation. "You dance with me."

They started dancing. Rachel, Angie, and Kristi went over to the table where Mrs. Bowen had set out punch, chips, and dip.

Randy and Bryan punched the decorations.

Jimmy sat on the sofa. Cassie went over and sat on the other end of it. Agatha sat beside her. Mike sat between Agatha and Jimmy. The four of them watched Brenda and Stacy dance.

Every once in a while Mike would look at Agatha. She'd look back, they'd both smile and then look away.

"Do you know how to dance?" Mike asked.

"A little," Agatha answered. "Do you?"

"A little." After a while, he said. "Do you . . . uh, would you like to go get some punch?"

"Sure," Agatha replied.

They both got up. Cassie watched them go over to the table and help themselves to the punch and chips. She looked at Jimmy. He shrugged. She shrugged back.

Stacy sat down on the couch next to Jimmy. "Whew," she said. "I need to sit down a minute. Boy! Dancing makes me thirsty." She looked at Jimmy. "Do you want to get some punch?"

"Not right now," Jimmy said.

Stacy tapped her hands on her knees in time to the music. "Good song, don't you think?"

Jimmy shrugged.

They sat side by side for a while without saying anything. "Well, I guess I'll go get that punch," Stacy said finally.

Cassie looked over at Jimmy. He had a surprised look on his face, which quickly changed to disgust. Cassie followed his eyes.

Agatha was dancing with Mike! "Oh, yuck!" Cassie said without realizing she was saying it out loud.

"You can say that again!" Jimmy agreed.

Cassie looked at him.

"Pretty weird, huh?" Jimmy said, curling his lower lip and hanging his tongue out. Cassie started to giggle. Jimmy tried not to, but couldn't help it.

"Very weird!" Cassie said, and they both laughed harder.

Cassie was surprised when Joel sat down next to her on the arm of the sofa. She hadn't seen him come in. "Good party, huh?" he said with a grin.

"Weird party," Cassie said, which sent her and Jimmy into another fit of laughter.

"I don't get the joke," her brother said, "but it must be funny to break you up that much."

Stacy walked over and stood next to Joel. She smiled at him, then at Cassie. "So what's the joke?" she asked. Brenda came up beside her.

"Nothing," Cassie said. "You wouldn't get it."

Stacy looked hurt.

"That's all right," Joel said. "I don't get it, either. We're probably too mature to understand their sense of humor. Right, Brenda?"

"Definitely," Brenda said.

"Yes," Stacy said, looking up at Joel, "definitely too mature." She took off her party hat and smoothed her hair down with her hand. Brenda took her hat off, too.

"You must be Cassie's big brother," Stacy said.

"Right," said Joel.

"Sorry. Stacy, this is my brother, Joel. Joel, this is Stacy, and you already know Brenda. Oh, and this is Jimmy."

"Jimmy the comedian." Joel grinned.

"It's really nice of you to let Cassie borrow your cassette player and all your tapes for her party," Stacy said. "I brought some tapes, too."

"Oh, yeah? What did you bring?" asked Joel.

"I'll show you." Stacy took his arm and pulled him away.

Cassie looked at Jimmy and they cracked up again.

"Definitely too mature," Jimmy said, slapping his leg. When he had calmed down he asked, "How come you're having dancing at this party, anyway?"

Cassie held up her hands and shrugged. Then she grinned. Then she put on a serious expression, lifted her chin, and said haughtily, "So we could all be mature."

They started laughing all over again.

The music stopped while Joel changed the tape.

"You guys look like you're having fun," Agatha remarked. Mike was right behind her.

"Speak for yourself," Cassie teased, still laughing.

Joel grabbed her hand. "Come on, kid. Let's show these guys how to dance."

Cassie hesitated, but Joel pulled her up. "Come on. One dance with your brother won't kill you."

Embarrassed, she let him drag her off the couch. He started dancing. For a few long seconds her whole body seemed to be frozen. She meant to dance, but nothing moved.

"Come on," Joel said. "You can do it. Just like the other night. Remember. Just kick, then step." He smiled reassuringly.

Cassie smiled back and started to relax. She picked up the beat and began to move. She felt like everyone was watching. "Ooops!" She stepped on her brother's foot.

"Maybe I should wear my combat boots," he said with a wink.

Cassie saw that Agatha and Mike were dancing again. Rachel and Angie were dancing, too, and Bryan and Randy were acting silly. They were flapping their arms like chickens and pawing the floor with their feet. Jimmy was eating chips. So was Kristi. Stacy and Brenda were watching and whispering to each other. Stacy never took her eyes off Joel.

Cassie grinned at her brother. He was all right sometimes. Too bad it wasn't her birthday every day.

When the song ended, Stacy came up to Joel. "You're a good dancer," she said.

"Thanks." Joel turned back to Cassie. "Thanks for the dance, kid. Have a good party." He started to walk away.

"Oh, aren't you going to stay?" Stacy asked with obvious disappointment.

Joel looked back over his shoulder, shook his head, and waved.

Stacy turned to Cassie. "Why didn't you tell me your brother was so cute!" She rolled her eyes and swooned.

"I thought you liked Jimmy," Cassie said.

"Oh, he's such a baby compared to Joel," Stacy said. "Joel's so much more mature. He's absolutely gorgeous! Don't you think so, Brenda?"

"He's okay. He's a big brat sometimes, though. Isn't he, Cassie?"

"Not so much anymore," Cassie said sharply. It was one thing for her to call her brother a brat and another to hear someone else do it. Especially someone who could be such a brat herself.

Mrs. Bowen came up and put a hand on Cassie's shoulder. "How about cupcakes and ice cream now? It's all set up."

Randy flew his spaceship cupcake, hovering it over Brenda's head. She giggled appreciatively, unaware that he had turned it upside down and was threatening to smash it in her hair. Other cupcakes made short flights, too, but inevitably ended up being eaten along with the ice cream.

Then Cassie opened her presents, thanking each giver and passing the gifts around to be admired and exclaimed over. After that the party was pretty much over and kids began leaving in twos and threes, as they had arrived.

"If I have a party, I'm definitely not having dancing, and I'm not inviting any of those dumb girls," Jimmy said, indicating Stacy with his thumb. "Just you and some of the ones who aren't so . . . crazy."

"You mean mature," Cassie said, putting her nose in the air.

"Right. Mature!" Jimmy said, shaking his head. "So long, Cassie."

"Bye, Cassie," said Mike. "Thanks for inviting me." He looked at Agatha. "See you at school."

Agatha nodded.

Definitely weird, thought Cassie.

When everyone had gone but Agatha, Cassie collapsed on the sofa with a sigh.

"Good party," Agatha said, sitting down beside her.

"Weird party," said Cassie.

"What was wrong with it?"

"Nothing," Cassie said with another sigh. "Stacy's just so boy crazy. Now she's all gaga over Joel. Brother!"

"Some of the boys aren't so bad," Agatha said.

"You mean, one of the boys isn't so bad, don't you?"

Agatha grinned. "Well, I noticed that you and Jimmy seemed to be having a pretty good time together."

"That's different," Cassie said. "We were just laughing. We're not all gaga."

"I'm not gaga. You sound like you're mad at me," said Agatha.

Cassie stared straight ahead.

"You're mad at me because I danced with Mike?"

"I never said I was mad at anybody."

"What's so bad about dancing with a boy? You danced with Joel."

"That's different," Cassie said. "He's my brother."

"Well, you talked with Jimmy and you were sure having fun laughing. What's so different about my dancing with Mike?"

"You think he's cute, right? And you like him for a boyfriend?"

"So?"

"So, I don't like Jimmy for a boyfriend. I just like him for a friend, that's all. None of this, 'Oh, he's so cute. Oh, he's so adorable. Oh, he's so wonderful. Oh, I wish I could marry him.'" Cassie swooned dramatically.

Agatha giggled. "Cassie, you're so silly. I never thought any of that stuff about Mike. Especially not anything like I wanted to marry him! I just danced with him a couple of times."

Cassie looked at her. A smile broke across her face. "I know," she said. "Just don't start going gaga on me, okay?"

"I won't," Agatha said. "I'm not Stacy, you know!"

The two girls sat side by side without talking for a few minutes. Cassie jumped when the telephone rang, but it stopped before she got to the door. She waited expectantly. Joel came out of the kitchen eating the birthday cupcake they had saved for him. "Who's on the phone?" Cassie asked.

Joel shrugged and swallowed his bite. "Somebody for Mom." He continued on his way to his room.

Cassie sank glumly back down on the sofa.

"Do you really think he'll call?" Agatha asked cautiously.

"Either that, or he'll just come to surprise me. I told you that." Cassie set her teeth and stared at the remains of the party decorations. Oh, why didn't her dad just call? This waiting was so hard. Oh, please, let him come, she prayed silently. Please, please make him come.

She blinked and let out her breath in a quick burst. Jumping abruptly to her feet, she declared, "I'd better start getting this place cleaned up."

"I'll help," Agatha offered, gathering some fallen decorations from the floor.

"I want to put those back up," Cassie said quickly. "I'm going to leave the decorations up so my dad can see them."

A worried expression crossed Agatha's face.

"Hey! I know what!" said Cassie. "You can spend the night! Then you'll be here for my whole birthday."

Agatha agreed, "I'd like that."

Cassie looked gratefully at her friend. Having Agatha there would make the waiting easier. "Come on. Let's go ask my mom."

Mrs. Bowen thought it was a good idea. "I'll call Amanda and see if it's all right. How about inviting her to come along on our picnic tomorrow, too? She's practically family now that you've adopted her as your 'Granny.' "

"Okay," Cassie agreed. "She'll probably be lonely if we steal Agatha for the whole weekend. Do you know where Joel is? I need him to get the ladder for me."

"I'm right here," Joel said, coming into the kitchen. "What are you going to do? Take down the decorations?"

"We're going to put some of them back up," Cassie explained. "Some of the boys knocked them down."

"Don't you think it's time to take them all down, now that the party's over?" her mother asked.

"But I want . . ." Cassie hesitated. "I want to keep them up for my real birthday tomorrow."

"You don't still think Dad's coming, do you?" Joel asked.

"Of course not," Cassie lied. "I can have my decorations up for my birthday anyway, can't I? Besides, Granny Gifford hasn't seen them."

Joel glanced at his mother. "I'll get the ladder," he said.

Cassie felt a strong urge to get away before her mother started talking about not being able to count on her father's promises. She took Agatha's arm and pulled her out of the room. "Come on. Let's get started."

When they were alone, Agatha asked quietly, "Your brother and your mom don't really believe that your dad is coming, do they?"

Cassie shook her head. "They're going to be the ones who are *really* surprised tomorrow."

Agatha picked up a couple of spaceships and untangled their strings. "Cassie?"

Cassie turned to her.

"What if your dad doesn't come?"

Cassie set her jaw and looked at her friend with a steady gaze. "You don't even need to worry about that," she said, "because he's coming."

The Picnic

Cassie was awake early Sunday morning. The gray light coming through the window told her the sun hadn't shown itself yet. Except for her, the house and everyone in it were still asleep. She rolled over and looked at Agatha in the sleeping bag on the floor beside the bed. Outside, the world was quiet, too, except for an occasional bird's twitter.

Inside Cassie Bowen it was a different story. Her whole body was wide awake and tingling in anticipation. Today she was ten years old! It was her very own day. A day for wishes coming true. She had only one important wish. A wish she wished with every ounce of her being.

She lay there, trying to be still but hoping Agatha would wake up soon, hoping her mother would soon get up and start making Cassie's special birthday breakfast of waffles with walnuts and grated orange peel. It was her dad's favorite breakfast, too. Would he get there in time to share it with her? Would he get there at all? She pushed her fear away. He *will* come, she told herself. He's just *got* to come.

In the distance, Cassie heard the sound of a car. Would it stop outside? Maybe. No. It faded away.

"Oh, please, somebody wake up," Cassie whispered. Agatha stirred, moaned a little, and went on sleeping.

Cassie sighed. She twitched her feet. She raised her arms above her head and made shapes with her hands. The light coming through the window changed from gray to gold.

Cassie heard a faint sound. A faraway sound. Was it another car? Maybe. Yes. Yes, it was, and it was definitely coming this way. It was on her street. Closer and closer. Cassie held her breath. It was almost to her house. It was to her house.

It was past her house, moving on down the street.

Rolling over, Cassie thumped her pillow and buried her face. Oh, where was her father? Please, don't let him be in California still. Let him be close—very, very close.

Wasn't anybody ever going to wake up? Cassie got out of bed and went into the bathroom.

When she came back Agatha was yawning and stretching. She grinned up at Cassie. "Happy birthday," she whispered.

"Thanks," Cassie whispered back. She went over to the window. "Look. The sun's shining. It's going to be a great day for a picnic."

Agatha propped herself up on an elbow and nodded. "I've never been to the lake."

"You'll like it."

"I know. I'm glad you invited me to come."

"Me too." Cassie ran to her bed and leaped into the middle of it. "Oh, I can't wait! I can't wait!"

Agatha jumped onto the bed and tickled her.

"No fair!" Cassie squealed. "It's my birthday!" She scrambled to bury herself under the covers.

"Hey! Cut the racket!" Joel yelled from the next room.

Cassie and Agatha stopped for a few seconds, looked at each other and burst into giggles.

"Good morning, birthday girl," Mrs. Bowen said, poking her sleepy face in the doorway and tying the belt to her bathrobe. "Good morning to you too, Agatha."

"Good morning," Agatha said.

Cassie ran over and hugged her mother. "Good morning, Mom."

"Are you hungry?"

"Ummm! For birthday waffles! My favorite!"

Mrs. Bowen smiled. "Coming right up."

Cassie ran back to the bed and pounced on Agatha, who tried to get under the covers as Cassie tickled her.

A pillow hit Cassie in the back of the head. She screeched and whirled around. Joel was standing in her doorway dressed in pajamas and armed with a second pillow.

"A guy can't even sleep in on a Sunday morning around this place," he said.

Cassie threw his pillow back at him. He caught it and held up both pillows with a menacing grin. She picked up her pillow and tossed it at him, but he fended it off with his own.

Agatha grabbed her pillow from the floor and heaved it. It hit Joel's elbow and dropped at his feet.

"Heh, heh, heh," he said. "Now I've got them all."

Cassie ducked, but not before the first pillow hit. Agatha grabbed it and was poised to throw, when she was hit.

For a few minutes pillows and screams flew back and forth furiously. Until, suddenly, Cassie and Agatha realized they had all four pillows and Joel was standing defenselessly in the center of the room.

Without a word they each picked up two pillows and jumped off the bed. Joel dashed down the hall, ducked into his room, and locked the door. Cassie slapped her pillow against the door a couple times before going back to her own room with Agatha.

Out of breath, they sank down on the bed.

"Whew!" Cassie said. "I guess that was my brother's birthday present for me. Beating us up with pillows."

Agatha laughed. "It was fun. My sister and I used to have pillow fights sometimes . . . before she went to college."

"You miss her, huh?"

"Yes. She's coming for Thanksgiving, though. I can't wait."

"She's nice." Cassie had met Agatha's sister when she had visited during the summer. "Come on, let's get dressed. I smell waffles!"

At breakfast, Cassie made sure she was sitting on the side of the table facing the window. She kept an eye on every car that went by, though she pretended to be completely absorbed in what was going on at the table. The waffles tasted wonderful, but as her anxiety grew, she found each bite harder and harder to swallow. When her mother offered thirds Cassie turned her down.

"What's the matter?" Mrs. Bowen said, only half joking. "You usually eat at least four."

"I guess I'm just too excited."

When Joel and Agatha had declared they could eat no more, Mrs. Bowen started to clear the table. "No chores for birthday girls or guests of birthday girls today," she said. "Joel will help me this morning."

"I'm a guest," Joel squeaked in a high-pitched voice. He bent his knees and put an arm around his sister. "Cassie and I are best friends."

Cassie laughed and pushed him away. "Come on, Agatha. This place is too weird." She led the way into her bedroom, but she felt restless in there. She couldn't see out front, and now that everyone was up, with the radio on, water running, and people talking, she was afraid she wouldn't hear if someone drove into the driveway.

So she took Agatha into the living room. Cassie got out a deck of cards and dealt a game of crazy eights, but she couldn't sit still and play. She kept getting up and walking to the windows.

"Why don't we just go outside," Agatha finally suggested.

Cassie nodded. "We're going out front, Mom. We'll just be walking."

Mrs. Bowen came in. "I've just about got everything ready. We have enough food for about eight people, I think. If you want to take a walk, why don't you go on over and tell Amanda that I'll bring the car and pick all of you up in about fifteen minutes."

Cassie's stomach lurched. Only fifteen minutes! That was hardly any time at all. "Maybe we should leave in half an hour. I'll call her and tell her we'll pick her up in a half an hour."

"If you want to wait that long. I just thought you were anxious to get going." She looked questioningly at her daughter.

Cassie avoided her mother's eyes. "We've got all day."

Outside, Agatha sat on the steps, but Cassie paced back and forth. "You're making me dizzy. Come on, let's walk if you can't sit still." Agatha took Cassie's arm and pulled her out to the sidewalk.

Cassie pressed her lips together and stared off down the street. Her father had a blue Chevy. At least he did when he left, but today he might be driving a rented car. The tightness in her chest grew as each approaching car went on past or stopped in front of some other house.

Joel came out on his bike and rode circles in the street. "We've got the car all packed. Mom said it'll be time to leave in about ten minutes."

"Did you get the chairs and the blanket?"

"Everything."

"Even the Frisbee?"

"Everything," Joel repeated.

Cassie surveyed the empty street and sighed heavily. Her throat ached as she turned toward home. "I guess we'd better go get our bathing suits and stuff," she said. "It's pretty warm. We might be able to swim later on."

Cassie was quiet as she stuffed her things in her beach bag.

Agatha watched her. "Are you going to leave a note?"

Cassie shook her head.

"It'll still be a good day," Agatha said softly.

Cassie just nodded. She didn't trust her voice.

Joel was standing with the car door open when the girls came out. "Front or back, kid?"

"Back," Cassie managed to say. She climbed in and scooted over to make room for Agatha.

"I'll have to get back there when we pick up Mrs. Gifford," Joel reminded them.

Mrs. Bowen turned to look at her before starting the car. "Are you okay, sweetie?"

"Fine," Cassie said, staring out the window at the tree beside the garage. She kept her eyes straight ahead until the car turned at the corner, and even then she allowed herself just one glance back.

Joel made the switch when they stopped for Granny Gifford, then they were off to the lake. The women in the front seat chatted pleasantly, but the back seat was ominously quiet. Once Joel tried singing a couple of lines from a popular song, really hamming it up. But Agatha's laugh was merely polite, and Cassie sat like a stone.

Her whole insides were aching and she felt like she was going to explode. Her thoughts tumbled in confusion and she didn't want to acknowledge any of them. It took every ounce of energy she had just to keep from crying.

When they arrived, Agatha exclaimed at the beauty of the lake and tried to interest Cassie in wading with her. Cassie just sat on a bench and gazed out over the water.

"Why don't you go on ahead," Mrs. Bowen said quietly to Agatha. "Maybe if she sees you having a good time, she'll decide to join you."

Agatha pulled off her shoes and socks and started for the water, glancing wistfully at Cassie.

"Wait, I'll go," Joel said, kicking off his shoes.

Cassie watched them hop and shriek as they stepped gingerly into the cold water. She and her dad used to race right in. She used to do lots of things with her dad at this lake. She fought back the tears.

Her mother sat on the bench beside her and put an arm around Cassie's shoulder. "I'm really sorry your plans didn't work out. Would you like to talk about it? It might help a little."

Cassie stiffened. She didn't want to talk about it. She didn't even want to think about it. This was her birthday. Her *birthday*, and she wasn't going to let her mother make her talk about being sad. "I think I'll go wading," she said abruptly, yanking off her shoes and socks. She ran to the beach, splashing straight into the water at Joel and Agatha, who screamed rewardingly.

"Don't think you can get away with that, just because it's your birthday." Her brother came after her, making great splashes with each stride.

"Agatha! Help me!" Cassie shrieked, turning to her friend for protection.

"Me?" Agatha responded. "You got me too, remember?" She grinned and splashed Cassie from the other side.

"No fair!" Cassie yelled. "Two against one!"

"That's the way *you* wanted it," said Joel. "Only I was supposed to be the one!"

In a few minutes the cold water had soaked through their clothes.

"Oh! It's freezing!" Agatha shivered.

"It sure is! How about playing some Frisbee in the sun while we dry off?" Joel suggested.

"Good idea," Agatha agreed. "I mean, if you want to, Cassie."

Cassie nodded. "I'm cold, too."

They found a sunny spot and tossed the Frisbee around for a while. Agatha tried to throw it behind her back the way Joel did. She looked pretty funny the first time, but Joel gave her some pointers and she got better. Then he showed her how to throw it under her leg.

"Come on, Cassie," Agatha coaxed. "You try. It's easy."

She did try once, but it was about all she could do to throw it the regular way. Her heart wasn't really in the game.

All three were good and dry by the time Mrs. Bowen called them for lunch. Cassie managed to eat enough so that her mother didn't fuss.

After lunch, Mrs. Bowen let the children rent a boat, making them promise not to take it out of sight. Joel and Cassie took turns rowing until their arms got tired. Then they let it drift.

Cassie lay on her stomach along the middle seat, bending her knees so she'd fit, and rested her chin on her hands. She waved to her mother and Mrs. Gifford. Joel lounged lazily in the front of the boat, and Agatha dangled her fingers in the water at the back.

The gentle rocking of the boat, the sound of the water lapping at the sides, and the happy voices of the few people on the beach soothed Cassie. She began to relax in the warm sun.

The next thing she knew her brother was waking her up. "Come on, Sleeping Beauty, we have to get this ship back to shore."

When the boat was returned, they put on their suits and went for a swim to cool off. The water felt good after the hot sun in the boat. As the afternoon passed, there were moments when Cassie actually forgot that her father wasn't with them, when she stopped wondering if he'd shown up after they left. In a way she hoped he had. She hoped he'd come and been terribly disappointed and hurt that she hadn't waited for him.

But the painful thoughts and jumbled emotions were all there as Cassie watched her mother light the candles on her birthday cake. What should she wish for? That her dad would be waiting when she got back? Or that she'd never have to see him again? Let *him* be the one to wait for letters and visits that never came.

Her confusion persisted while everyone sang "Happy Birthday." Taking a deep breath, she tried to push all thoughts about her father away. She blew out all ten candles in one fierce *whoosh*.

"You get your wish!" Agatha cried.

"Good," Cassie said, "because I wish we'll still be best friends on my next birthday."

"You're not supposed to tell!" Agatha gasped. "But don't worry. It'll still come true." She squeezed Cassie's hand.

Then Cassie opened her gifts. Mrs. Gifford had knit a pair of rose-colored slippers for her. "Oh," Cassie exclaimed, "just like the ones you made for Agatha!"

"Except mine are blue," Agatha said.

"Thank you. They're beautiful!" Cassie gave Granny a warm hug.

In the next package Cassie found a cassette tape from her brother. She turned it over curiously. She didn't want to seem ungrateful, but it seemed strange that he would give her a tape when she had nothing to play it on.

Joel grinned. "I thought you might want to practice dancing some more."

"Thanks," she said.

"I'll let you play it on my cassette player sometimes," Joel offered. "Just be sure you ask first."

Cassie smiled broadly. This really was a generous gift, if her brother was willing to share his precious cassette player. "That's great! Thanks." She hugged him awkwardly, and his ears were red when she let go.

Agatha handed Cassie a small package. Inside was a bracelet they had admired together when they were shopping for school things. "You got it! You remembered all this time! Oh, thanks!" Cassie gave Agatha a hug. "I'll let you borrow it sometimes."

Last, Cassie opened the presents from her mother. One box had two new pairs of pants. "I mostly got those because you needed them," Mrs. Bowen explained. "You're growing so fast these days! I just thought it would be more fun to wrap them up."

"Thanks, Mom. I like these colors." Cassie reached for another box. In it she found a really cute sweater with tiny rabbits knitted into the design.

"Oh-h-h!" Agatha exclaimed. "The colors go with the pants. Look, Cassie." She held the pants up next to it.

"It's really cute, Mom. Thanks."

"You're welcome." Mrs. Bowen handed her the last gift.

Cassie opened it to find a small glass jewelry box. The top had a design of pressed wildflowers. Cassie stroked it gently. She was pleased that her mother had chosen such a grown-up gift for her. She set it down carefully and went to give her mother a hug. "Thank you, Mom. I'll keep that forever."

"You're welcome, sweetheart." Mrs. Bowen looked proudly at her daughter for a few seconds, then clapped her hands together. "Well, who wants some cake?"

In spite of her resolve not to think about her father, a tightness crept into Cassie on the drive home, and she crossed her fingers. It was getting dark when the Bowens pulled into the driveway after dropping off Agatha and her grandmother. Cassie peered around anxiously. Her slight hope wavered. There were no cars in sight.

As she helped carry things in, she kept her eyes open for a sign, a clue that someone had been there while they were gone. Maybe there would be a note.

Her mother caught her looking around the living room. The decorations were beginning to droop. "Have you seen the TV schedule?" Cassie asked, hoping to divert her mother's attention.

"It's right on top of the television."

"Oh, yeah." Cassie picked it up and made a show of opening it to see what was on.

"I know it's your birthday," her mother began, "but tomorrow is a school day. Don't you think you should go in and take a bath?"

"Sure." Cassie tossed the schedule aside and walked briskly down the hall.

One Day at a Time

In her room, Cassie spread her presents out on the bed. She wondered if it would be too warm to wear the sweater to school tomorrow. Probably, but she'd wear it anyway. She'd wear a blouse underneath, so she could take the sweater off if she got too hot.

She stroked the jewelry box and put it right in the center of her dresser, slipping the bracelet and the tape inside. Then she picked up the new slippers and her nightgown and went into the bathroom.

Numbly she undressed and turned on the tap in the tub. As the water ran, she looked at herself in the mirror. "I'm ten," she said aloud. "Today I'm ten . . . but Daddy . . ." She couldn't finish her sentence. The words just wouldn't come out. Saying them aloud would make things too real.

She slipped into the tub, the warm water rushing

in around her. The pain she'd been holding in all day swelled inside her until it finally overflowed. Tears ran down her cheeks, slowly at first, then steadily as she sobbed, "He didn't come. He really didn't come. It's my birthday and he doesn't even care."

She sat in the tub for a long time, her salty tears mixing with the bath water. How could her own father do this to her? After he promised. After she wrote and practically begged him to come. After she told her mother and Joel and Agatha that he'd be there for sure.

It was like that other time, the time he promised to take her and Joel camping for a week, and they got everything they needed and packed it up and were supposed to go the very next day. But her dad came home and said he was going on some fishing trip with his friends instead. He said they'd go camping some other time, but they never did. She'd cried that time, too. So had Joel. No wonder her brother didn't want her to count on their dad. He'd tried to warn her. So had her mother, but she wouldn't listen. How could she have forgotten about that time? How could she be so stupid?

There were other times, too, when her dad had promised something and changed his mind at the last minute. But this was the worst of all. This was her birthday. Cassie cried until it didn't seem like there were any feelings left inside of her.

She shivered in the now-tepid water, splashed the last of the tears off her face, and got out.

Her mother and Joel were sitting in the kitchen when Cassie appeared. Joel was having another piece of birthday cake.

"You look all cozy," Mrs. Bowen said. "Those are nice slippers, aren't they?"

Cassie nodded.

"Do you want some cake, too?" her mother asked.

"Just a little piece." Cassie used her thumb and forefinger to show how thin.

Her mother cut a slice and passed it to her. "I hope it's been a nice birthday for you."

Cassie felt the tears welling up again.

Mrs. Bowen swished the tea bag in her cup. She seemed to be trying to find the right words. Cassie took a bite of cake.

"I'm sorry your father didn't come. I know it's a big disappointment," her mother finally said.

Cassie picked at the crumbs on her plate. She felt like such a fool. Her face was getting hotter and hotter, especially behind her eyes. "I guess I'm not hungry." She pushed the cake away, stood up, and hurried out of the room.

"Cassie," her mom called after her.

Cassie ran into her room and closed the door. She threw herself across the bed and let new tears come. She heard the door open and close softly and footsteps cross the room to her bed. She expected her mother's voice, her mother's hand to reach out to try and comfort her. But it was Joel's voice she heard instead.

"Hey, I'm really sorry, kid. I mean, I felt kind of creepy last summer when he didn't show up for my birthday, too. But it's not like it's your fault, you know, or mine either. Even when he lived here, he wasn't too great at keeping promises. Remember that camping trip? And all those times when he'd say we'd do something special on Saturday, and we'd get all excited, then Saturday would come and he'd say he was too busy? Remember that? It's his problem is what it is." Joel put his hand on Cassie's shoulder.

"Come on, don't feel bad, Cass. We're real lucky we've got Mom, you know?"

Cassie nodded, her face still buried in her pillow. She couldn't stop crying. Joel sat there a while longer. Finally he got up.

The door opened and closed and thinking she was alone, Cassie rolled over. She was surprised to see her mother standing there. Mrs. Bowen stepped toward her, holding her arms out. Gratefully Cassie accepted them and pressed her teary face into the warmth of her mother's shoulder.

Her mother stroked her hair, making soothing sounds as she rocked her child back and forth on the bed. "I love you, Cassie. I wish there was a way I could make it not hurt so much."

"I hate him," Cassie choked out. "I hate him."

"You really feel angry with him right now. It hurts a lot."

"He didn't even send me a present! Not even a card, Mom! He could've at least sent me a card! He could've called me. He could have at least told me he wasn't coming. I hate him! I really hate him!"

"I don't know if you can understand this, Cassie," Mrs. Bowen said, "but as sorry as I am for you and how much you are hurting, I'm even sorrier for your father. He's hurting himself, too. He's letting himself miss being with you, seeing you grow into a very special young lady. I wouldn't miss that for the world." She kissed Cassie on the top of the head.

"He doesn't think he's missing anything! He doesn't even care!" Cassie's poor body shook with angry sobs until she was finally spent, and relaxed limply in her mother's arms.

Mrs. Bowen shifted slightly. Cassie tightened her hold. "I love you, Mom," she whispered. "Thank you for giving me a good birthday." She looked up at her mother and smiled weakly through her tears.

Mrs. Bowen kissed Cassie's forehead. "I love you, too, funny face. Forever and ever."

The next day in school Cassie's new sweater and bracelet were admired by all the girls, and her party was still the big topic of conversation.

Stacy especially wanted to know all about Joel, and Brenda wanted to know if Agatha was "going with" Mike. She said Cassie should ask Jimmy to ask Mike if he liked Agatha. Agatha just made a face at Brenda.

Cassie didn't really feel much like talking to anyone, except maybe Agatha. She felt sort of drained and empty inside. The tears were gone but not the hurt. She was glad when school was out.

"I think I'm just going to go home today," she said as she and Agatha neared the corner. "Is that okay?"

Agatha nodded. "Come on over later if you feel like it."

Cassie glanced at the mailbox but walked on into the house. Joel was standing in the kitchen, and Cassie's eye caught the stack of mail on the counter. She looked at Joel, who shook his head.

"He's really being a creep about this," he said, putting an arm around his sister. Gratefully, Cassie leaned her head against him for a few seconds. Then she sighed audibly and stood up straight.

"Well, too bad for him," she said bravely.

"You know it!" Joel thumped her on the back. "We're the two greatest kids in the world!"

"Right!" Cassie marched into her room. PeeWee was lying on the floor. "So we're a year older," she said, picking him up. "How does it feel? I guess it's some good and some bad. I wish . . ." Cassie set her bear on the corner of her desk and gazed out the window. "I wish more wishes would come true."

The birthday card finally arrived on Wednesday. A ten-dollar bill fell out when Cassie opened it. She picked it up, then read the note her father had scribbled at the bottom of the card.

I'm really sorry I missed your birthday, Punkin. I hope you aren't too disappointed. I've been pretty busy and just couldn't get away this time. I'll make it for sure next year. That's a promise.

> Love and Happy Birthday,
> Daddy

Sure, Cassie thought angrily, I know about your promises. She checked an impulse to tear the card up and throw it away. Tearing up the card wouldn't change what had happened this year or what would happen next year either. But maybe it *will* be different, she thought, and even if it's not, maybe it won't hurt so much.

Cassie put the card on her desk and the money in her new jewelry box. Then she went over to the Giffords' for a game of Parcheesi in the tree house with Jimmy and Mike.

The next evening, Mrs. Bowen announced that Lyle Kester had invited the three of them to pizza and a movie Friday night.

Cassie cringed inwardly. Why did her mother want to keep seeing that guy? Hadn't her father already been trouble enough? Why couldn't it just be the three of them? She could count on her mother and Joel. They kept their promises. Who knew what would happen if they got involved with . . . with Lyle Kester . . . or anybody else?

Joel and her mother waited for Cassie to say something. But Cassie didn't want to say what she knew they wanted to hear.

"Come on, Cass," Joel coaxed. "He's okay, and the movie is supposed to be great."

Cassie studied her mother apprehensively. "Do you really like him?"

"He's very nice, and I've had a good time when I've been with him."

"Are you going to marry him?"

Mrs. Bowen looked shocked. "I'm not even thinking about that, Cassie! I'd have to know him a lot better before I was ready to make that kind of decision. We might see each other a few more times and find out we really don't have that much in common. Besides, I'm not sure I'll ever get married again . . . and if I do, you'll have plenty of advance warning. I promise. Let's just take things one day at a time, all right?"

"Starting with pizza and a movie tomorrow night?"

"Starting with pizza and a movie tomorrow night," her mother said.

"All right," Cassie agreed.

"All right, kid!" Joel reached over and mussed her hair. "You're going to love the movie!"

"That's what you say!" Cassie smoothed her hair and poked her brother in the ribs. "I'll tell you whether I love it or not, *after* I've seen it . . . *kid*!"

APPLE®PAPERBACKS

Pick an Apple and Polish Off Some Great Reading!